Lost in Cat Brain Land

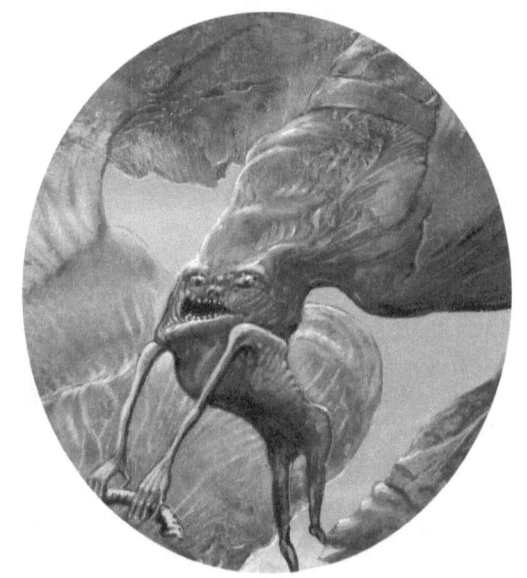

CAMERON PIERCE

Eraserhead Press
Portland, OR

ERASERHEAD PRESS
205 NE BRYANT
PORTLAND, OR 97211

WWW.ERASERHEADPRESS.COM

ISBN: 1-936383-04-7

ACKNOWLEDGMENTS

"Holiday Sings the Egg Dilemma" first appeared in *Bust Down the Door and Eat All the Chickens,* "Death of a Dog Eater" first appeared in *Esteban's House of Bizarro,* and subsequently in *Dark Recesses,* "The Depressed Man" first appeared in *Verbicide Magazine,* "A Scorpion Town in California" first appeared in *The Dream People,* "Broom People" first appeared in *Nemonymous #10,* "Embryo Tree for Android" first appeared in *susurrus: the literature of madness,* "How to Live Forever" first appeared in *The Dream People,* "Flowers" first appeared in *Bust Down the Door and Eat All the Chickens,* "The Green Monster and His Loneliness" first appeared in *Bare Bone,* "I Am Meat, I Am in Daycare" first appeared in *The Horror Library Volume II,* and subsequently in *The Magazine of Bizarro Fiction,* "Crazy Love" first appeared in *The Journal of Experimental Fiction.*

Printed in the USA.

AUTHOR'S NOTE

I received my first story acceptance when I was sixteen. It sold to The Dream People, the online bizarro journal founded by Carlton Mellick III. Flash forward five years and I'm having beers with Carlton at Concordia Ale House in Portland, Oregon. I had recently compiled this collection, but it didn't have a title. Carlton suggested Lost in Cat Brain Land, after the Melt-Banana song "Cat Brain Land." It was perfect. A few months before, I'd gone to a Melt-Banana show dressed in a banana costume and lost my glasses in the mosh pit. So this book is dedicated to Melt-Banana and Carlton Mellick III, a friend, mentor, and great writer. It's also dedicated to the next person I punch in the face. Today is my birthday. Maybe I will be the next person I punch in the face, or maybe I'll just drink some beer and crash my bike into a tree.

– Cameron Pierce, May 23, 2010

P.S. Special thanks to the following people: Rose O'Keefe, Jeff Burk, Alan M. Clark, Richard Tingley, Kirsten Gwin, Mykle Hansen, Jeremy Robert Johnson, Gina Ranalli, Forrest Armstrong, Kevin L. Donihe, Bradley Sands, D. Harlan Wilson, Andersen Prunty, Jordan Krall, Chrissy Horchheimer, Kevin Shamel, Daniel Scott Buck, John Edward Lawson, Jennifer Barnes, Royce Icon, Tony Perone, Dr. Joy Hardiman, Matt LaFever, Justin Walker, Byron Alexander, Ryan White, Jon Howard, Chris Cardenas, Elizabeth Tyning, Montana Salvoni, Gabriel Majeski, Rafael Dwan, Lily Greeniaus, Nick Cato, Steve Sommerville, John Skipp, Brian Keene, Olympus Found, my instructors and fellow grunts at Borderlands Boot Camp, and my parents. If I missed you, please don't break my neck.

TABLE OF CONTENTS

CAT BRAIN LAND

for Albert Camus

Tanuki died today. Or maybe it was yesterday. I can't be sure. I found his carcass in my bed this morning. His black fur was matted with blood, his white chest no longer white. When I tried to pick him up, the gray Egyptian cotton bed sheet came with him. He'd bled a lot and was glued to the sheet. I didn't sleep in my bed last night, so maybe he died yesterday.

I wrapped him in the sheet and carried him to the kitchen. I set him on the kitchen table, unwrapped the sheet, and stepped back. I observed the dead cat in a detached manner perhaps ill-suited for the situation, but my emotions had turned to shit over the previous days, over Ann. I was finally starting to calm down today. I'd gone dead inside, at least. I wasn't about to work myself into another mental apocalypse over a dead cat, no matter how much I loved the cat; no matter if this meant I was alone without even a cat to love me, with Ann on her way out.

I rubbed Tanuki's left ear between my thumb and index finger, just the way he liked it when he was alive. His pink tongue poked out of his mouth. It'd blackened at the edges. His eyes bulged, as if in the last seconds of his life he had seen something that attracted and repelled him immensely. His pupils had burst. They'd spilled into his bloody scleras like

7

runny black egg yolks.

The cat had taken to hunting mice in the fields at night. He probably got caught on the wrong side of a scuffle with a coyote, hawk, or particularly aggressive rattlesnake as he returned from a hunting trip. I bet it took the last of his strength to climb into bed. I bet he expected to find me, thinking I would help him or at least hold him in my arms as he passed away.

Well, I didn't help him. I let down my only friend. Maybe we could have helped each other, but it was too late. Too late for him, too late for me and Ann. I petted the cat and told him I was sorry. I asked him why he chose today or yesterday to die. He'd lived to inconvenience me. It's how he showed his love. Ann expected me at The Frog Bar in an hour. I'd have to call and cancel. She, of course, would be pissed. No sympathy from her, not over my dead cat. Not the way our relationship was going. I didn't even know where she was staying.

How goddamn sorry I was for both of them, for the things I'd done or failed to do.

My body longed for a hot shower. I felt dead cat germs scuttle in an out of my pores like ants in tunnels of dirt. I reached my right arm over my shoulder, stuck my hand down the neck of my wrinkled black dress shirt, and scratched between my shoulders. I scratched my neck and behind my ears. I scratched my scalp. With my left hand, I scratched my belly and below my beltline. No matter how much I scratched, the dirty itch remained. My shirt was covered in cat hair, Tanuki's hair, so I took it off. I was not wearing an undershirt for reasons I could not place. I always wore an undershirt.

I scratched my chest and studied Tanuki. He smelled pretty bad. I must have jostled his decaying molecules when I picked him up. I wanted to slip away for a shower, a long, hot one, but my legs rooted me to the floor. Tanuki was dead. I held a moral obligation to stop thinking for myself and figure out what killed him. How in the hell did these things happen anyway? Why did cats die? Why did *my* cat die? "Oh Christ get over it," I said to myself. "You know better than anyone how these things happen."

I fetched the heavy duty, food grade scissors from the knife rack on the counter. I turned back to the dead cat on the kitchen table, snapping the scissors open and shut as I stood over his body. Before deducing what killed him, I needed to cut him away from the sheets. It was simply impossible to tell what killed him when fabric concealed one side of his body. His hair had grown long and wild. It would be easy to cut away. I often told him that he looked like a furry black cloud. He would brood under the kitchen table—his favorite place to brood was under the kitchen table, on which he now lay—and hiss at me or Ann when we walked by. I would turn and tilt my head back and laugh, "Look at the furry black cloud getting angry now!" Or Tanuki might hop into bed at night. He'd step lightly across the blankets and knead his paws into my chest, purring. The shadows of my hands would vanish into the plush darkness of his fur, and I'd whisper, "Furry cloud. My furry black cloud."

He was a stiff cloud now. His black fur was as brittle in some places as uncooked spaghetti; it even snapped under pressure. *A dead cloud.*

I wedged the scissors between his body and the sheets and snipped his fur, careful not to cut into him.

A few minutes later, they separated. I set the scissors on the table.

Now that I'd freed the cat of the bedding, the prospect of inspecting his ruined body and uncovering what destroyed him made my knees bend inward. I felt ruined myself, like I'd awoken into the worst sort of hangover, the sort that followed the nights I went for it all, breaking shit and starting shit, fucking up anyone in any way I could, verbally or with my fists and other ways, it didn't matter, so long as it prevented me from getting my hands on myself.

The nightmare feelings of the past few days returned. They came back very sudden, and far worse.

My heart and guts flopped like trout suffocating on a sandy bank, fish whose lungs were ripped and flayed by golden treble hooks that some fisherman yanked out with a scowl and a shrug, because everyone knows trebled barbs don't budge if you're tender and gentle with fish that swallow the hook. My heart and guts felt like those fish, except I didn't swallow the hook. It had been shoved down my throat, and my brain felt so much worse. I was standing in the doorway of a breakdown with a dead cat and soon-to-be-ex-girlfriend pushing at my back.

I steadied myself against the kitchen table. I closed my eyes and inhaled deeply of the foul air. I inhaled and exhaled in rapid succession. My breaths came up shallow. Whiffing death gave me sea legs and the spins. I started hyperventilating.

I tore myself away from the table, eyes watering, and stumbled over to the kitchen counter. I slid a drawer open and grabbed a brown paper bag. On my knees, I held the mouth of the bag tightly over my own mouth and tried to remember how to breathe.

Soon, my inhalations deepened; my breathing stabilized. Brown paper bags worked wonders against hyperventilation attacks.

As I stood, crumpling the bag into a ball, my phone vibrated in my pocket. I took it out and looked at the name and number on the screen. It was Ann, likely calling to flake out or to make sure I wasn't I planning on flaking. Our habit of always canceling on each other had created rifts in our relationship from the beginning.

"Tanuki died," I said. Not giving her the courtesy of a hello.

Silence.

"I found him in our bed. I don't know what happened. There's a lot of blood. I can't come out tonight. I can't talk. If there's anything you want to say to me, say it now because everything is fucked anyway. So say what you want to say and let me go." I was crying into the phone.

More silence on her end.

"I have to take care of my cat," I said.

"I'm coming over," Ann said. She sounded upset, like she could barely get the words out.

She hung up.

I set the phone on the counter, debating whether to call her back. I desperately needed a shower, a shave, fresh clothes, food, sleep, to clean the wrecked house, and to get Tanuki somewhere else before Ann arrived. If she walked in the door and saw the dead cat on the kitchen table, she'd flip. As bad as I looked, figuring out what killed Tanuki was top priority. No amount of showering and grooming would erase the dark circles beneath my eyes or make my sallow, gaunt face appear any healthier. I could expect Ann to remark upon my physical state. *You look like shit*, she would casually observe.

The cat was more important. I looked tired and hellish, but I still might learn a thing or two about Tanuki's death and feign, for a little while, that everything was under control.

Pressured by the unknown time constraint, I returned to the table. I braced myself for the worst and flipped Tanuki over, disclosing the side of him I had not seen. I leaped back and shouted, "Fucking Christ!"

A wide gash ran the length of his side, just below his ribcage, as if someone had gutted him with the claw of a hammer. The hairless flesh clinging to his broken ribs was singed. They'd burned him. They'd gutted the cat and burned him.

I held my breath and stepped closer. I was prepared to wrap him up in the sheet and bury his body right then. I could make up a story to tell Ann. Maybe someday I'd even believe that other story myself. I hoped so. When I paid witness to the full extent of the damage, the gutting and burning seemed like child's play. The world had transformed into a monstrous elephant and it was doing a fine job of stampeding my ass into the fucking ground.

In my first take, I'd missed what was going on under his ribs. I put my head up close. I wasn't sure what the insides of a cat were supposed to look like, although I knew they weren't supposed to look the way Tanuki's insides looked. It appeared that whoever or whatever killed him had removed his interiors and filled him up with brains. Tiny, pinkish gray brains. Cat brains.

My cat was filled with cat brains.

The brains glistened under the harsh fluorescence of the overhead light. They were a gelatinous refusal of the stiffness and unswayable lifelessness of the cat himself.

The cat brains quivered.

Were they parasites? Were they alive?

I backed against the counter and groped around behind me for my phone.

I watched the brains without batting an eye as I flipped open my phone. I cast my eyes down only long enough to make sure it was connecting to Ann. Seeing the little screen light up with the caller ID photo of her, an image of her laughing and stomping on a sand castle we'd built at Pismo Beach last summer. I stepped up to the table again, hovering over Tanuki, and observed the brains.

Pressed against each other in the canyon-like gash, the cat brains mewed, although they had no mouths.

Ann answered on the third ring.

"What is it?" she said.

I opened my mouth to urge her to stay away, but before I got a word out, two yellow cat eyes blinked open on the surface of a cat brain. And then eyes opened on all the brains I could see, and I knew that every brain inside the dead cat had awoken.

"Holy shit," I muttered, dropping the phone.

I heard Ann shouting on the other end of the line.

I bent over and reached for the phone. I had it in my hand when a skinny black paw closed over my right wrist and buried claws into my flesh. I dropped the phone. I looked over my shoulder and saw that the paw was appended to a furry tentacle.

A cat tentacle.

I flailed my left arm blindly, battering air. I dropped to my knees, still cuffed around one wrist, and grabbed my dress shirt off the ground. I whipped the shirt over my shoulders to distract my assailant so that I might break their hold on my right wrist.

"Help! Send help!" I shouted, hoping Ann was still on the phone. It was facedown on the floor right in front of me, but my left arm swung the shirt uncontrollably, automatically, out of pain and anxiety.

Another clawed tentacle dug into my right leg and flipped me onto my back. I saw from this position that the cat tentacles protruded from the brains inside Tanuki's body. Although I was sprawled out on my ass, facing the tentacles head-on gave me a little confidence that maybe I could break their grasp and escape. I wrapped my left hand around the skinny tentacle now pinning my right arm to the floor, but as I wrenched back on the tentacle, trying to pry my right arm free, two more tentacles unfurled from the dead cat. They seized my left arm and left leg, then began folding my limbs inward, as if to make them meet in a point over my torso.

I screamed out as my joints cracked and my muscles contorted. The four cat tentacles proceeded to lift me up.

I teetered precariously above the kitchen table as the tentacles bent into impossible pretzels. They swung me into the fluorescent light and glass rained down on the table. Weak light streamed through the window above the sink and the sliding glass doors that opened the living room onto the balcony and overlooked the Pacific Ocean. The sun had not yet disappeared. It was like the ghost of an over-easy egg howling on the watery dark horizon, so many miles from shore that nobody except the seabirds and sea creatures could hear it howl.

That ocean sunset was the last thing I saw before the tentacles folded my body into a human cube and stuffed me inside the corpse of my cat and down through many layers of cat brains.

Eventually the cat brains ended, and I fell.

I hit a spongy bottom. I inspected myself for injuries. My wrists and ankles bled from where the tentacle claws held me. No damage from being folded into a cube. My limbs moved fine. I stood and gazed upward, trying to estimate how far I'd fallen. A light that seemed to emanate from everywhere all at once cast everything in a pinkish gray haze.

The cat brains floated above like clouds.

Brain clouds.

The furry tentacles coiled around some clouds. Their paws drooped, swaying in midair, as if the cat tentacles had gone to sleep.

I lowered my gaze and scanned my surroundings. Brain cacti jutted up here and there. I wiped my brow, realizing how much hotter it was in here. Despite the wetness of the brains, a dry, arid wind rolled across the land, sweeping vagrant particles of brain to the air. So this cat brain land was a desert.

I spun around and around, looking for a sign to point me in some direction. Looming in the distance, in a ring surrounding the desert: gargantuan mountains of brain, with peaks like twisted pink daggers.

I kept looking.

A dark figure sat at the base of a cactus like a little death doll, but as I approached, I made out a patch of white on its chest.

"Tanuki!" I shouted, and broke into a run.

My dead cat was alive inside of himself. For the moment, that made it okay that I'd been abducted and pulled into his desecrated body by a set of cat tentacles. For the moment, all I wanted was to hug my cat. Tears streamed down my cheeks. Blood gushed from the puffy claw marks that serrated my wrists. Tanuki's presence made everything feel okay. I wanted to nuzzle his nose against mine and tell him I loved him. I wanted to hold my ear to his body and listen to him purr. Most of all, I wanted to assure my furry black cloud that we would never be away from each other again. Living in Cat Brain Land with my best friend would be so much better than the isolation I was pressed up against. The only thing missing here was Ann.

About twenty yards separated Tanuki and I.

Fifteen.

Ten.

Closing.

And then he ran.

He turned and dashed away from me, across the desert. I tried to follow him, but the harder I ran, the deeper my feet sank into the brain floor. Weighing no more than ten pounds, Tanuki sped gracefully across the mushy ground. It probably felt like a trampoline to him. To make things even more futile, I was out of breath. My heart thundered in my chest, threatening to explode. I collapsed beside the cactus and pressed my face against the ground where he'd sat just moments ago.

I opened my eyes some while later, having passed into a half comatose state, when the brain clouds mewed, followed by a shriek that penetrated Cat Brain Land from the outside.

"Ann!" I cried, instantly springing alert. My voice was drowned out by the mewing of the clouds.

The cat tentacles snaked up the clouds, rising to get Ann, I was sure.

Groggy, a little breathless still, but powered by a manic force, I ran.

After a while, I slowed down. I stood about right where the cat tentacles disappeared, but they were still above the sky. I couldn't scream anymore. I was battered and exhausted. I had to face that I could not reach out to Ann. No matter if I screamed myself, I was not going to reach her. She was not going to hear me. I could not save her from the cat tentacles.

The tentacles reappeared. A doll-like object fell from their paws, a doll-like object I knew to be Ann, but as the paws released her, her legs fell separately from her body, as if the paws had torn her apart at the waist.

Her disconnected halves landed a few hundred yards ahead. I rushed across the desert to meet her, and although the distance was short, every step was a drunken stumble. I wobbled and staggered. My bones were flimsy and weak. I couldn't breathe. Ann lay perhaps a hundred yards ahead when my knees finally gave and I collapsed. She saw me and called my name. I called back to her. She started crawling toward me, dragging her legless body across the jellylike ground. No longer possessing the strength to stand, I crawled to meet here.

And I told myself that we would stick together no matter what.

No matter if we were lost in Cat Brain Land, no matter if we'd been horrific and inhuman to each other for a long time, we remained two people who once loved one another more than anything, and somewhere, in the desert or the mountains beyond, we had a cat to find.

Holiday Sings the Egg Dilemma

I'm in the living room of an apartment that isn't mine, making small talk with a woman who has vomited into the same bucket for at least half an hour. She says it's her dog. She swallowed her dog and now she wants the crawly bastard back. That's what she calls the dog. A crawly bastard. The apartment does not belong to her or anyone she knows. "But I'm not concerned," she says.

"Why should you be concerned?" I say, because these things happen.

"But I'm not," she says, and she pukes some more.

This is how I'm spending my last day on earth. Tomorrow, the World of Friends will arrest me and ship me to a slave outpost on Venus. I know this because the WoF sent a letter last week notifying me that I had been selected for their Venusian slave program, and that I should not try to escape or alter my sentence because the World of Friends only has my best interests in mind, and because they will find me if I make a run for it. Being a slave is a dream, they say. I'm supposed to take their word for it, and why wouldn't I?

A paw emerges from the woman's mouth. She heaves

once more and a scruffy brown head pokes out, spreading the woman's lips until they crack and bleed at the corners and someone's knocking at the door.

"Who is it?" I shout.

"World of Friends, open up," a man's voice. I have never met anyone from the World of Friends and wonder if somehow this apartment and the woman and my imminent detainment have some common factor linking them together. "Open up," the voice repeats, louder.

I walk across the room but stop short of the door. What if it's all a practical joke? Rule #6921 in the Friendly Fascist Handbook says that standing in the same room with the World of Friends is punishable by death. I look through the peephole but it's blocked. I say, "What about Rule Six-Nine-Two-One?"

"You're forgetting Rule Seven-Four-Eight-Seven," the voice says.

Rule #7487: Negligence to permit the World of Friends entrance into any room is punishable by death. I shrug. I guess it doesn't really matter which rule I break if I'm scheduled to be deported tomorrow anyway. What the hell.

I open the door and am immediately sprayed in the eyes with mace. "Holy shit!" I scream, but it's a garbled version of it that comes out. "It burns," I howl, "I'm blind!"

I stumble back from the doorway and trip over the woman choking on her dog, which barks as I hit the floor. "To ensure your personal safety and that of the World of Friends," the man says. He must be standing above me but I'm too busy scratching my eyes out to notice. The dog barks again.

Finally, I can make out a blurry fractalization of the room. The woman is coughing up blood and the dog laps at the red puddle with its long tongue. The man from the World of Friends turns out not to be a man at all. He, or it, is a chicken. A regular goddamn chicken. It kicks the can of mace away from me and I wonder how it managed to spray me in the eyes or hold the mace at all. "Jon Ito," the chicken says, "your deportation to Venus has been deferred indefinitely. You have been chosen to eat the last egg ever eaten legally before the anti-egg act takes effect nine-o'clock sharp tomorrow morning. Are you in your current condition fit to appear on international broadcast, or should we sentence you to death?"

"Wait a minute," I stutter, "What's going on? I don't understand."

"The World of Friends has awoken. There will be no more egg-eating in the universe, not under our jurisdiction."

"You mean that you're all a bunch of chickens, and you've been asleep all this time we thought we were being controlled and monitored every second of the day?"

The chicken pecks at my nose. "Your tactics of deception will not work on us. Television or death. Choose now."

I shrug. "Television, I guess."

The woman still bleeds and her dog still laps at the blood as the chicken drags me out of the apartment by the hem of my pants.

I pick up the silver four-pronged fork.

This is it, the last egg ever eaten by creaturekind. I set down the fork and pick up the glass of cinnamon-spiced whiskey. The chef, another chicken, pecks at my ankles. "Don't rush me," I tell him. "You can't imagine how hard this is."

I had watched the chicken fry the egg on medium heat in garlic-seasoned olive oil, dropping from its beak dashes of rosemary, thyme, basil, and shrimp extract. The idiots should know I'm allergic to shrimp, but they say nothing. On the drive from the apartment to the studio, I learned more about the anti-egg act from the squad car radio. As of tomorrow morning, the Tasmanian mongoose can no longer suck on the yolks of exotic birds without risking serious jail time. Fishes small and large can no longer eat the eggs of other fishes, be they small or large, without a hand-slap from the World of Friends. Now they're forcing me to eat the last egg ever eaten legally on live, international broadcast. And when I walk offstage and the crowd goes wild, they're going to shoot me.

The executioner pecks at a corncob behind the velvet curtain, only the fabric separating him from the audience. I know he's there and that he's eating corn because I passed him as they directed me onstage.

I sip at the whiskey. Within seconds of swallowing the last bite of egg, they're going to kill the cameras, usher me backstage, and then the guard will shoot me with the .44 magnum strapped to his back. Five-million chickens have their beady eyes poised on me, and that's only the ones packed inside the stadium. I wonder if any humans, any that I know, are watching from home, if they haven't already been shipped to detainment camps. "Fuck," I say, but not loud enough for even the chef to hear.

It's not that I hate eggs, but I don't like them either, not particularly. An occasional omelet is fine, but the texture of eggs—over-easy, scrambled, hard-boiled, anything—never suited me. I chug what remains of the whiskey and bury my face between my hands. The audience clucks louder, a manic steady drone like a factory of wind-up monkeys. I wonder how that woman and her dog are doing. Still bleeding/licking, probably. Or maybe the dog turned on the television after I left and now they're watching me sweating up here, getting pecked by the chef and squawked at by five-million chickens who all look exactly alike.

And then it strikes me.

I don't have to be this man, Jon Ito. Wherever I came from, or whatever I might think of this egg dilemma I'm in, all that matters is the mysterious apartment housing a woman and her crawly bastard. Not that I want to return to that living room and smell her vomit, because even if that's what I wanted to do, it might prove impossible to escape the studio and navigate my way through a city potentially unlike any I have ever seen prior to the awakening of the World of Friends (which happened way too suddenly for my taste).

No.

What it means is that this stadium and the apartment are the same place. I am Jon Ito only because I choose to be in the living room of an apartment that isn't mine, or at least because the World of Friends chose for me to be there.

The egg on the plate opens its yolk mouth and speaks. It says, "This is the condition Deleuze called schizophrenia, and you know what happened to Deleuze." And then there is no egg mouth.

"Who the fuck is Deleuze?" I ask the chef.

The chicken shits on my sneakers as the crowd squabbles louder than ever. For a moment I'm relieved that I never suffered from social anxiety, but then again, maybe I do. Right now I'm having a nervous breakdown. There are no chickens anywhere (except they're everywhere), there are people watching me and these people love me (for god knows what reason), there is no such thing as the World of Friends (there could be nothing without the World of Friends). Sweat runs down my face like you wouldn't believe. I don't know what's happening anymore. I get this idea that I should rip off my face but this is crazy. No matter how apeshit the world goes, you've got to know better than to rip off your own face. Jon Ito would know this. Who can I be now that I'm gone? It's a distant voice in my head that I feel approaching, growing. It tells me to rip off my face, to unleash the yolk explosions, that everything will be fine soon enough. Since I want everything to be fine, I decide to do it . . . to someday claim this new voice as my own.

I start by plugging my nostrils with my thumbs and then steadily pull up, up until the cartilage busts and I'm breathing blood. The chef flaps his wings as a red-slick yolk pops out of the hole in my face and splatters across the chicken's back. I can't say how I came to have yolk in my face, but whatever the yolk is made out of melts the chicken into a puddle of bones, feathers, and one red-and-white checkered apron.

Plop-plop. I separate my slippery flesh like vaginal lips and more yolks pop out, floating toward the audience. The yolks break on the chickens in the front row first. Further back in the stadium, fleeing chickens clog the exits. Excess yolk leaks from the hole, which is now fist-sized. It crusts over my eyes and mouth and forms a yolk mask and I smile. Whatever happens next is totally up to me. John Ito never died. He is going to be born very soon.

This is the end of the line for me.

I'm a yolk-faced mess in the same strange apartment, watching myself birth yolks from my face on the television. The dog yacks up something awful in the middle of the living room, blocking my view of myself. "Could you move a little to the right?" I ask.

The dog pauses mid-vomit. "I've swallowed my woman," he says. "Woof."

I turn up the volume with the remote control since I really don't want to touch the sick dog or act like his blocking my view is such a big deal, which it kind of is. It's not every day that you find yourself destroying the creators of the universe on international television. A human arm emerges from the dog's mouth and someone knocks at the door. The World of Friends is dead and the other fascists are still fighting for power, so no law can compel me to open the door this time.

Whoever it is knocks again, louder. There isn't any peephole so I can't see who it is first.

A second arm forces the dog's mouth wider than it should go and reminds me of a video I once saw of a python swallowing a baby hippo.

"I hear the television. I know you're home," a man's voice.

"It's not my home," I call.

The woman's head, the same woman who swallowed her

crawly bastard, pops out of the dogs mouth. The dog can't take it anymore and it dies. "Just open the fucking door," the woman says. She might be the reason for all of this, and so I obey.

I unlock the door and open it. Standing there is not just a man, but a man-woman attached at the hip by a giant egg. "What's this?" I say.

The man-half of the man-woman says, "I'm Bart Starr." As he says this, I scrutinize his sagging, maggot-crawling flesh and vintage Packers jersey. Hell, maybe he is Bart Starr.

"Nice to meet you," I say, sticking out my hand and worrying about the maggots. I realize that the man-woman has no arms and withdraw my hand, worrying that maybe I already offended them/him/her by offering an impossible handshake.

Bart Starr nods his head at the woman, who appears to be catatonic. He says, "This is Billie Holiday, straight from heaven and with one last song just for you. Can we come in?"

"I don't do religion," I say.

"Let's play catch," Starr says. He pushes past me into the apartment, dragging Billie with him. "Nice place you've got here. Too bad you've got to come with us when the music's over."

I glance at the television just to make sure the footage of me is still playing so that Bart and Billie know they're not the only ones who have claimed their hour of fame. Too late. I'm no longer there. It's now an episode of Doogie Hauser. I always hated that show despite never seeing an entire episode. Regardless, I don't think the boy doctor normally cuts nurses' tongues out with a scalpel and then stitches chicken fetuses in their place, which is what he's doing right now.

"You a fan?" Bart asks, kicking at the dead dog with his foot.

"No," I tell him, leaving no question about it. Apparently the woman died before crawling entirely out of the dog, so they're bloating there together in the middle of the living room, taking up space.

Bart shrugs, looks at Billie. "Let's get this rolling," he says, and punches the egg.

The egg cracks and Billie Holiday gets sucked through the crack and into the egg. The crack seals itself and the egg appears good as new. "That should do it," Bart says. "Rub that egg with good lotion while I use the restroom."

But Bart Starr doesn't use the restroom. He instantaneously dissolves into a writhing heap of yolk, no different than my face. Then the television blinks out and Billie Holiday sings from somewhere far inside the giant egg, which rests on the pile of Starr yolk. She's singing about being in an apartment that isn't hers and making small talk with strangers and more than ever I want to leave this place. For the first time I also get the feeling that I have always lived in this apartment and that I am finally approaching the heaven in the gloomy center of it all, into that Venus where the World of Friends always wanted me to go, where the disembodied voice emanating from nowhere reminds me that free will is a lie, singing the same song, the same strange song that pushes me beyond the lips of the sun and into fireworks of afterbirth. Now a choking newborn writhes on the floor in a pile of dog and woman, an almost-embryo greedy to fill itself by sucking the yolk from my skull, by sucking me dry.

Visitor Ganesh

He hates fish. Jack hates fish and that goddamn Marybot cooked
fish.

I grab the teakettle off the stove burner, fill three mugs with
hot water and sprinkle a handful of instant coffee granules in
the three mugs. The trout frown up at me from the pan. For
three weeks that robot has cooked nothing but fish for lunch
and dinner. "Jack doesn't eat fish," I call.

Marybot slides into the kitchen on her bicycle wheel-legs.
She buttons her white blouse. "He can eat it or starve. I didn't
have time for groceries," she says.

Once again, I wonder why I married an android.

I pick up one of the coffee mugs and walk out of the kitchen.
"I haven't seen Jack in ten years. The least we can do is show
him a decent meal." It's useless. She can't know what a decent
meal feels like, but most people don't anymore, not since the
FDA pressured the Feds into making it illegal for anyone to live
in a residence that possesses less than seven microwaves.

"I'm sure you two will have enough to talk about that he
won't mind fish. I even made cinnamon rolls for dessert. Have
you met anyone who could resist my cinnamon rolls?" Maybe
she's right. Jack was always a talker, and Marybot does make
damn good cinnamon rolls.

"It's been so long." I sit down at the table, on one of the

mounted boars that my senile father gave us in place of dining chairs. "Hell, I never expected to hear from Jack again. I don't understand why he called today, of all the other days he could have called."

Marybot cycles out of the kitchen. She pulls up her skirt and sits on the boar across from me, her eyes narrow slits. Her eyes glow green, the way all android eyes glow when they're scanning for information to fill in their incomplete data. "I guess that's why you never mentioned him to me," she says.

"High school was a long time ago," I say. I don't like talking to androids about the past, not even Marybot. "He sounded so different on the phone, I almost didn't believe it was Jack."

"People change," Marybot says, as if this is a natural thing to her. "Think how different you and I were when we first met." I do. I think of that shit-eating grin on Dr. Blight's face as he presented me my very own android to love and cherish and honor until death catches up with me or someone disconnects her wiring.

The doorbell rings. I get off the boar and walk into the living room. I peer through the peephole and there, on the other side, stands Jack. Scrawnier than I remember, dark circles ringing his eyes. Must be struggling with a recent breakup, I figure. A divorce? Anyway, Jack looks pale and too skinny. It's too bad we won't be able to show him a decent meal.

I unlock the door and open it wide. This version of Jack reminds me less of a former classmate and more of my own father in his last days fighting a losing battle with liver cancer.

"My God, Jack, you're hardly more than a skeleton."

Jack shrugs. He blinks dazedly.

"Come on inside," I tell him, "dinner is ready."

"I'm Marybot," says my wife.

Jack nods but doesn't shake her outstretched hand. He sits down on a boar but doesn't pick up his fork or knife.

Marybot has already placed the trout on the table. The sweat feels hot under the stained glass lamp hanging from the ceiling. Is he one of those people who's prejudiced against androids? Is it the boars? "It was nice hearing from you," I say. "I admit being shocked hearing your voice on the line. What have you been up to these past . . . oh hell, I guess it's close to eleven years since graduation."

"I have been well," Jack says.

"We've got time, so tell me everything," I say, sipping at my coffee and realizing I forgot the other two mugs in the kitchen.

Jack's eyes dart around the dining room and kitchen.

"You've got a nice place," he says.

I fake-smile. An awkward tension settles over the room. It's eating me alive. "Marybot teaches at Wasson High and I'm a supervisor at G.C. Dickenson, the same distributor we stole cases of beer from back in high school. On weekends I work at the Barnes & Noble they built last year. Have you seen the new shopping center?"

Jack nods. "I remember G.C. Dickenson. Didn't know they were still operating. These places are all so strange to me."

Marybot swallows a bite of trout. She glances nervously at me and says, "Walt said you don't like fish. I would have made something different had he told me before."

"Trout is fine," Jack says. "I lived in a cabin by a river for six years. Out there by myself, without a grocery store for miles, I caught many fish. Trout is fine."

"Was it that same cabin your family owned? I remember you talked about moving up there someday," I say.

"The same cabin, that's right. Out near Bishop. Even when I lived up there, I never had electricity, and sometimes I fell asleep with the lantern burning. One of those nights, I don't know how this happened, it got knocked over. The cabin burned to ash. How I failed to wake sooner and how I put it out when I did, not even God knows. I guess some things are meant to be while others aren't."

"Christ, I'm sorry to hear that," I say. "Where did you go?"

Marybot sets down her fork. "What do you mean some things aren't meant to be?"

Jack still hasn't touched the trout. His silverware sits on the red napkin where Marybot placed it when she set the table. "Have you got some whiskey?" Jack asks.

Marybot stands and wheels into the kitchen. She returns with three glasses and a bottle of Knob Creek and I pick up my mug to find that the coffee has grown cold. Marybot pours the bourbon, filling each glass perfectly half full. "No matter how hard up things get financially," I say, because I have to say something, "a man needs quality whiskey. You can't settle for the cheap shit. It isn't good for the heart."

I tip my glass toward Jack and take a sip, feeling like a moron as the alcohol prickles my tongue and throat.

Jack gulps half the liquor and slams the glass on the table. He wipes his mouth on his flannel sleeve, closes his eyes, and says, "These years since the cabin burned down, I have been going places."

I pick at the fish on my plate. I peel golden-pink flakes of meat off the trout's ribcage with my fingers. Marybot slaps my hand. "Don't be a child," she says.

Ignoring her, I ask Jack, "What do you mean you've been going places? What places?"

Jack downs the other half of whiskey. "I have been here, there, and everywhere else. Now I'm here with you."

"I made cinnamon rolls for dessert," Marybot says.

"Why don't you bring them out?" I say, staring down at my plate.

Jack refills his glass and gulps more whiskey. The glass slips from his fingers and falls to the table. He cradles his head between his hands. "I'd like to tell you my story," he says, "and I want you to listen hard. I want you to listen like you've never listened before, because there are things men should never know, and if they come to know these things, they should only tell them once."

I look up from my plate and right at Jack, almost right through Jack. Yet the man just holds his head in his hands. Marybot narrows her eyes at me. I look away from her. This is already getting to be too much.

Jack raises his head. Something shimmers in his eyes. He isn't crying and his eyes aren't watering and since I don't know what else can make eyes shimmer like that, I say nothing and try not to feel one way or another about it.

"I'd like to tell you my story," Jack says.

"Then go ahead," I say. "Tell your story and we'll listen."

"It isn't all as simple as that," Jack says.

"What do you mean?" Marybot says. "Walt, what does he mean?"

"I mean that when one tells a story, the telling isn't as simple as black and white. What is told is largely determined by the particular relationship between teller and listener. What you hear, Walt, may be very different than what your wife hears, and it may affect each of you in contrary, conflicting ways. There is truth in what I say, but there are lies. You cannot beat a horse to death with its own beating heart. Trust me, I tried. You cannot love another if they don't offer the proper sacrifices at your altar of lies, or else the tiny truths that bind you together all unravel. I loved a woman once. Another time I killed a man. I found no enjoyment in the act of killing. I found no enjoyment in the act of loving. For me, they are the same. There is truth in what I say, but also lies."

I look at Marybot. "Get those cinnamon rolls," I tell her.

"I want to hear this," she says.

"I told you to get those cinnamon rolls."

"And I told you I want to hear this."

"Can't you hear me in that metallic head of yours? Get into the kitchen and let me speak with Jack alone."

Marybot shuffles into the kitchen. She slams a cupboard. The faucet begins to run.

"I apologize for that," I say, sipping at the whiskey. "Marybot and I love each other very much and we never fight. I hate doing it, laying down the law like that. It reminds me of my father."

"Sometimes there are no laws," Jack says.

I make to set down my glass but think better of it. I sip at the whiskey instead. "Jack, what's this you said about killing a man? Since we spoke on the phone, I sensed something was wrong. You've said a lot of strange shit since walking through that door, and that couldn't have been more than an hour ago. I know everyone's mind gets tired at some point or another, and if that's it, if you've been saying these things because you need a little vacation, just say so. I remember you having a good heart. I won't hold tonight against you. So tell me, what's this about murder? What happened to you?"

"I've been so many places and now here I am."

I refill mine and Jack's glasses. "How did you manage to visit all these places when you claim to have spent so much time in the same cabin?"

"I had my first visit in the cabin," Jack says. "Ganesh was my first visitor, but there are so many more just like him."

"Are you saying a man named Ganesh visited you and that you visited all these places while living in the same place? I don't know what to say," I tell him.

"Then say nothing at all."

The Tiffany lamp hanging above the kitchen table casts half of Jack's face in green shadow. The other half could have been hammered out of tin. Straight out of a Faulkner story.

Jack's eyes blink out at me from their wrinkled cavern of his flesh-papered skull, almost pleading, and very much like the abandoned Adelaide mine we used for a clubhouse as children.

"Tell me about Ganesh," I say.

"Ganesh isn't important," Jack says, as casual as if we were discussing classmates or past loves or any of the good old times.

"Then why the hell did you bring him up?" I say, feeling the blood rush to my face, the veins in my neck swelling.

Jack sips his whiskey now, the way good bourbon was intended to be drank. He opens his mouth to say something but sips more whiskey instead. He repeats this (open, sip, open, sip, open, sip) until he holds the glass up to the light, a pin's head of liquor at the bottom glistening in the glass like it was all made of something primordial and infinitely more delicate than gold.

"Ganesh is only one of them," Jack says, lowering the glass. "They're all quite the same, really. Is there more whiskey?"

"Who are *they?*" I whisper, because some things can only be spoken properly if you whisper them, and I suspect this might be one of those things.

Jack reaches across the table and grabs Marybot's whiskey. "If your wife isn't going to drink this, I hope she won't mind me helping myself."

I wish Marybot was still here at the table. Maybe I could call her in and we could eat cinnamon rolls and go anywhere but where the sick feeling in my head tells me this conversation is going. Jack always had a penchant for things that were no good for him.

"That's better," Jack says. "Now *they*, if you're going to put it that way, *they*. . . ." He guzzles the whiskey and wipes his mouth on his flannel sleeve. "You want to know what they look like, where they come from, or what intentions they've got?"

"Anything," I say, furious, "all of it. If we're talking about extraterrestrials, just go for the whole shebang. Just tell me whatever it is you've got to tell me."

Jack nods. "I can't tell you where they come from because I'm not so sure myself. Ishtar visited me in the cabin. Others followed, but there was never much rhyme or reason in their coming or going. I lived with one for a while. She's the woman I loved. The man I killed, his name is Ganesh. He lives inside me now."

"Hold on a minute," I say. "Slow down. I'm not following. A woman? You said they all looked the same, and what's this you're saying about killing the man who visited you? Was he some sort of intruder, Jack?"

"They do look the same. That is, until you search inside them. Anyway, they can't be from outer space. If I had to describe them, and you're the first one I've admitted this to outside my journal, the visitors look like fleshed hogs."

I recall that Jack's father had been a taxidermist, the same one who stuffed the boars we're sitting on. This already stank of an Oedipal complex.

"Except," Jack continues, "it's more like the corpses of crippled humans dug themselves out of their graves and, discovering that they still couldn't walk, decided to kill pigs, hollow 'em out, and then wear their flesh until it melded to their bodies. Their croak is like . . . dead dogs laughing. I have no idea what kind of image that puts in your head. I wish I could do a better job describing them to you. I wish I could."

As he speaks of these visitors, Jack loosens up. Despite the apparent lunacy in everything he says, his demeanor reminds me more and more of the old Jack. Maybe the whiskey is just working its magic. Maybe Jack staged this elaborate joke and is losing the steam required to carry on with it. His description of the creatures could have surfaced from the horror films he obsessed over as kid, or straight out of his father's workshop. If I had to guess, I'd say it's some warped fusion of the two. At least Marybot is still in the kitchen. She'd be having nightmares for weeks. Androids are more vulnerable to nightmares than we are.

"The visitors love fish," Jack says. "They love fish so much that they do special things to the humans they meet, and they do very special things to the humans who love them, and if you kill a visitor, well, I can show you Ganesh."

"What are you saying?" I ask. I need more whiskey or some other means of forgetting this visit ever occurred.

"Let me show you what they do to humans they meet," Jack says. He slides his boar from the table and bends over to untie his shoes. He pulls his right shoe off and then his left shoe.

I stare at my dinner plate and then back at Jack's feet. Where his right foot should be, and where his left should be, flop eyeless trout crawling with white maggots. I swallow to refrain from puking up the trout and whiskey.

"This is what the visitors call Standard Procedure," Jack says.

I want to scream. I want to hold Marybot's hand. I want to call the police and let them know about this gnashing, violent lunacy eroding the flesh of the world.

Jack stands on his fish feet. He unbuttons his flannel shirt and lets it hang loosely, revealing a stained tank top beneath. "Call your wife in here," he says.

I stand. My shotgun sits in the closet at the end of the hall. Marybot could dial the police from the phone on the kitchen wall. I could call to her. I could dash for my gun and call to her. But for what reason? To what avail? If there are monsters in the world, then they exist within a man's mind. They are the troubles a man causes and the troubles committed against him by others. That a man struggles with monsters says something about his character. It says he is weak and sick and that he cannot endure the battle waged by every human between good and evil. This, I think, is what Jack has become. The fish feet are part of some elaborate costume, his story an indication of his inner psychotic landscape, and now the time has come for him to leave.

"I asked you to call your wife," Jack says.

And so I call to her.

They replaced Jack's heart with a rusted treble hook. Each barb extends the length of a grown man's index finger. "This is what they do to those who fall in love," Jack says, holding his heart

33

out for me and Marybot to inspect.

I study the hole in my old friend's chest. A black, eyeless eel dangles from one of Jack's nipples. When Jack pinches the eel's tail, it stiffens into a slender doorknob. According to Jack, this convenient access into his chest cavity benefits the visitors and himself greatly, for the treble hearts are still in prototypical stages and demand constant modifications. Jack believes that someday all humans will have such hearts, or so he tells me. Marybot faints after reaching out a trembling hand to touch the rusted hook.

"You need to leave," I tell Jack.

"You haven't seen Ganesh," Jack says.

I point at the hook and say, "Get your heart back inside your chest and leave. I'm calling the police."

Jack tugs on the eel and hangs his heart from one of the spongy cables twirling inside his body. He seals the flap of flesh that serves as a door, strokes the eel's head, and sits down on the boar where he had drank whiskey and eaten none of the trout. "How about those cinnamon rolls?" he says.

"Get out or I'm calling the police," I say, moving toward the kitchen. Stepping over Marybot, I hesitate. Should I leave her on the floor like that?

"Call them," Jack says, "but you won't like what they say."

"Why is that?" I say. I think of the shotgun sitting in the closet at the end of the hall.

"Get me a cinnamon roll. We'll talk."

My guts grumble. The fish isn't settling. More whiskey might solve that, but a peculiar gleam in Jack's eyes troubles me. Why should I *not* call the police? I don't want them to discover that the shotgun is unregistered, for one. And then there are the illegal knives I brought back from Mexico. They're in a cigar box on the top shelf of the den closet, along with the marijuana for when my back aches. But all I want is for this maniac to leave. Is that such a crime?

"How about those cinnamon rolls?" Jack says. "And some

more whiskey, if you've got it."

Nodding, I enter the kitchen. The swinging door settles, closing me off from the visitor. I lean against the refrigerator and close my eyes. The phone hangs on the wall across from me. I know that. To the right of the phone, and to the left of the electric stove, sits the tray of cinnamon rolls. In the cabinet above the stove, I know there's another bottle of Knob Creek. I open my eyes. It's a bad idea to leave Mary passed out on the floor and alone with Jack, who has a rusted treble hook for a heart. Stepping across the small kitchen, I open the liquor cabinet, grab the bourbon, and with the other hand scoop up the cinnamon roll tray.

As I reenter the dining room, I drop the cinnamon rolls. Where Jack sat now rests an elephant's head. There is no body attached to the head, and the elephant head appears to have been born without flesh or turned inside-out.

"Sit on a boar," says the elephant head. Its crackling voice possesses no qualities I associate with voices.

I sit on a boar and open the whiskey bottle. I pour a drink for myself. Even if the elephant head wants whiskey, I don't know how it could hold a glass without any arms or legs. I slam the bottle on the table a little too loudly and tip back my glass. I wipe away the whiskey that dribbles down my chin. Marybot groan-whirs on the floor. I hope she doesn't wake up.

"Pour me a glass," says the elephant head.

"What did you do with Jack?" I ask.

"I replaced him. Pour me a glass."

"Tell me your name," I say.

"They call me Ganesh," says the elephant head.

I pour another glass of whiskey and slide it across the table. "The same *they* that visited Jack?" I say.

"The ones who worship me," Ganesh says.

The elephant's trunk slaps and gropes around the table until it latches onto the glass. Suctioning onto the side, Ganesh lifts the glass above himself and then turns it over. Bourbon splashes over his red, meaty skull and drips onto the carpet. I realize that the elephant has no eyes and yet feel that Ganesh possesses some other sense that allows him to see, perhaps much more clearly than I myself can see. I catch myself thinking of the elephant head as a *he*.

I want to protest about the spilt bourbon. I want to rush down the hallway to where the shotgun rests, if only to splatter the wall with my own brain pulp. To forget.

The whiskey surges through me. It warms my belly while the trout refuses to settle. All in all, I felt the need to vomit up more than just the dinner. The entire evening, maybe, and maybe this entire life. Was this Ganesh speaking? Was this Ganesh controlling my thoughts?

"I haven't killed a man," I say. "You can't get inside my head. *I haven't many of them and they don't exist.* None of you can hurt me."

Ganesh laughs. The laughter possesses no qualities I associate with laughter. "I heard of a man you murdered. I may have spoken to him. He is the man you used to be."

I recall what Marybot said. How different we had been when we first met, as if androids can change or grow (can't they?). I shake my head. "It's not a crime," I say. "That's life. Nobody could survive if they didn't change. It's called adaptation. Humans would have never made it so far if we didn't change. Hell, we probably would have died out during the ice age or something."

Ganesh says, "The crime is that you believe in the lie. You are guilty of being human, and therefore you are guilty of murder. Middle-aged, Earth is now on her death bed. You are the reason, the sickness. Now you will shed your human shell and be remade in my image."

In the kitchen, the phone rings.

"Hello?" I say.

After the caller blabbers on for a while, I set the phone

down and walk out of the kitchen. "Ganesh, it's for you," I say. At my feet, Marybot murmurs but does not move.

"But no one knows where I am," Ganesh says.

"Maybe someone followed you," I say. "Or at least they followed Jack, knowing you were inside him. Anyway, it's for you."

The elephant head shifts uneasily in his seat.

I'd be willing to bet the elephant head is incapable of leaving the chair and too embarrassed to admit it. "Want me to take a message?" I say.

"Can you?" Ganesh says, sounding relieved.

In the kitchen again, I lift up the receiver. "Ganesh is busy. He said to leave a message. Who is this?"

On a yellow notepad, I scribble a name, brief message, and address. Without saying goodbye, I hang up the phone. Before going back into the dining room, I open the fridge and grab two beers. I need something to take off the whiskey edge, not to mention this entire visitor fiasco. For the first time, I wish I was schizophrenic. To have been so blessed, like my younger brother Richard, and to have pills to numb the lunacy away. To have been so blessed.

Fuck blessedness.

"I got you a beer," I say. I place the beer and yellow post-it note in front of the inside-out elephant head.

Ganesh's trunk finds the note and slobbers on it for several minutes while I drink my beer and return to the fridge for another. When I come back to the dining room, Ganesh is splashing beer over his own head.

Discarding the can on the floor, Ganesh says, "I must go. God has been taken hostage by guerillas in Africa."

"That was God on the phone? What do the gorillas want with him? More bananas?" The message the caller left is utter gibberish, so he must be lying or bullshitting.

"Guerillas as in guerilla warfare. God is not Charlton Heston, and this is not Planet of the Apes. Help me from my throne."

"Can't you turn back into Jack?" I ask.

"I am not Jack," Ganesh says.

I recoil at the thought of putting my hands on the blood-slick beast. "It's just that I wouldn't be much help in getting you to—"

"Nevermind," says Ganesh, cutting me off. "Can I have this boar?"

I'm almost drunk, but I realize that Ganesh is offering to leave, and so I tell Ganesh to have them all, have all the boars in the house.

"What would I do with so many boars?" Ganesh says. "Could I ride them all at the same time? Could I build a Mount Krishna out of boars or a Boar Land for the children? Could I punish you for being stupid?"

"I just meant—"

"You cannot prevent me from taking this boar. I am immortal."

I wonder what immortality has to do with stealing boars. Probably not much, except drunk with my brother one time, around the onset of his illness, we dug up a tree from a grocery store parking lot and carried it home. The tree still lives in our parent's backyard.

"Here I go," Ganesh says, "taking the chair."

"Go for it," I tell him.

Ganesh raises his trunk and blows a kazoo sound. Black horses, scaly and legless, slither out from where his eyes should be. The two horses coil around the base of his trunk. They open their mouths and blast flesh-textured rainbows into the boar, which melts into a four-legged puddle of coarse hair and taxidermy parts. Having apparently completed their duty, the horses slither up the elephant's face and back through the pinkish, empty sockets. The boar puddle solidifies around Ganesh and the elephant head now possesses four spindly pig legs. Bowing, Ganesh wobbles to the living room's front window and jumps out. The only evidence of a visitor is the broken glass.

And still, Marybot slumbers on the floor.

Shortly after Marybot regains consciousness, the phone rings again. It's an old friend of hers from Dr. Blight's laboratory and she wants to have dinner tomorrow night. She wants to keep better contact with all her friends from back home, this android says. I tell Marybot no. We will not have this woman as a guest, not even for a single evening. I'm surprised when Marybot agrees with me. "All we need is each other," she says, and squeezes me tight as the phone rings again.

It's Bill. The last time I spoke to him was high school graduation. "Come on out for a beer," he says. "I'm only in town for a night. You remember Jill Cassidy? We got married. Are you married? Bring your wife if you're married."

"I'm sorry," I tell Bill, truly almost sorry, "but tonight is not a good night."

"Why? What's wrong?" he says.

I hang up the phone as Marybot leans against the kitchen counter, looking worried. Before either of us can say anything, the phone rings again. "You answer it this time," I say.

She answers the phone without saying anything. The caller says something and then she hangs up.

"Who was it?" I ask.

But she won't tell me. She turns away and wheels out of the kitchen. As I follow her down the hallway to our bedroom, the phone rings again. "Tell me who it was," I call, but she has already slammed the bedroom door and pushed in the button lock.

The phone rings all night. Marybot says nothing but I can hear her breathing when I put an ear against the door. We are too afraid to answer the phone anymore and too afraid to disconnect it. At some point, I walk into the kitchen and grab another beer from the fridge. The glowing numbers on the microwave catch my eye. It's four in the morning and the phone continues to ring. For some reason this is enough to make me cry and I slump down against the base of the refrigerator and the phone rings and I sob louder than I have in a long time. The visitor is gone but the effects are just beginning. I don't know how or why this is happening, let alone what *is* happening, and this makes me more afraid. I think Marybot knows something, or maybe the caller after Bill said something, and I hope that soon she will come out of the bedroom so we can make some order out of this mess. If we have to disconnect the phone, we disconnect the phone, and if it takes something else, then by god we'll do it because this is our life. If we let go of each other then all we've got is this being afraid, but maybe it is too late now to ever pick up again without being afraid. We've got to hold on. Without the consolation of warm machines, who would we be when we look out the window at dawn? How would we know that's who we are, or is it already too late for that?

DEATH OF A DOG EATER

Pike passes the sign-in sheet to the lady on his left. He stands. The fold-up chair beneath him scrapes against the floor. He waves at the people sitting in chairs. "My name is Pike Fischer," he says. His forehead and underarms drip sweat.

"Hi Pike," the people say.

"How can we help you this evening, Pike?" says Deidra, a mid-fifties woman with a badge that says CHORDINATOR pinned to her red overalls.

"I like to eat dogs," Pike says.

The crowd gasps.

"This isn't Dog Eaters Anonymous," Deidra says. Her eyes glow red. Deidra is a robot. "Do you have a problem with alcohol? We are here to help people struggling with alcohol."

Pike licks his lips. He reaches for the lip balm in the pocket of his frayed jeans. He applies cherry-scented lip balm as he says, "I eat dogs."

"Dog eater!" A John Candy look-alike rips a fake beard off his face and approaches Pike.

"Sit down, Ronnie," Deidra says.

Ronnie throws the beard in the air and swings at Pike, but he misses. Pike falls to the floor anyway. The fake beard lands on his face. Ronnie grabs his own chest and collapses next to Pike.

"He's having a heart attack!" somebody shouts.

"Seize the dog eater!" somebody else shouts.

They lift Pike off the floor. He applies lip balm. He came here to get help, not kill people.

The people release Pike.

"Yuck," somebody says.

"He smells," somebody else says.

They run away pinching their noses. Pike is happy that he can't smell himself. Otherwise he would probably be dead. But he's sad that he emits an odor so terrible that sometimes it kills people.

"Leave," Deidra says, "and never come back to this place!" She's the only one remaining in the room with Pike.

"I need help," Pike says.

"Get out before I call the police."

Pike leaves the Alcoholics Anonymous meeting. He feels dejected and angry. "Stupid recovering alcoholics," he says. He wipes his eyes, then gets a good idea. He smears lip balm on his eyelids. He feels just like an overstuffed vacuum bag, happy that he tried, hoping for another shot.

He gets in his car.

He drives his car down Gosford Lane.

He stops at a red light.

He turns on the radio.

He turns off the radio.

The light turns green.

"Green means go," he says.

He works up the nerve to go.

He goes.

He's in the middle of the four-way intersection when a truck speeds through the red light and smashes into the side of his car.

Sometimes a minute takes an hour to pass.

The ambulance is bright. It takes Pike away.

"I've got you babe," he shouts.

The ambulance people are freaked out a little bit. Pike

isn't thinking about them. He is thinking about the dog in his freezer. "I've got you babe," he shouts. He can practically taste the terrier's frozen eyes.

"Some people deserve to be sick and wounded," one of the ambulance people says.

"Some people belong in the hospital," says the other.

It takes one listen of The Cure's Love Song to arrive at the hospital.

They pull up to the emergency doors and take Pike out of the ambulance. He is very worried about all the blood spilling out of him. He is also worried because the ambulance people are trying to soak it up with paper towels.

"Don't you have anything better?" he says.

"These are double absorbent," one of the ambulance people says.

"Double," says the other.

"You don't need to emphasize it," the first ambulance person says. "Surely he knows what double absorbent means."

"You always say something twice when it refers to a deuce. Oreo Double Stuffs? Double. Double the trouble? Double. Double Mint Gum? Double."

"Double shut up before I double punch you in the double mouth."

"Double. Double. Double."

"Double, double! Double, double!"

The ambulance people break into a slapping fight. Pike feels very dizzy. His elbows tingle. He licks his lips and closes his eyes.

When the world moves so fast, time and space cease to matter. We're standing alone in a room with death, and we have always stood in that room. With dead dogs crawling up the walls. Grinning dead dogs. Our dead dogs.

In Heaven, Pike Fischer marries a poodle. He sets out to relive the same horrors all over again.

THE
DEPRESSED MAN

A man walks into a grocery store. He forgot his shopping list at home. He picks up a green basket and walks into the produce section. The lighting hurts his eyes. Fruits and vegetables rot, he thinks. He will not buy them. He gazes at potatoes and wonders if other shoppers notice his apathy toward them.

The man wanders into the bread aisle. Bread must have been on his grocery list. He usually enjoys sandwiches, but he will not buy bread. He has not enjoyed sandwiches for some time. Protein will boost his morale. He walks away from the bread.

He shuffles up and down the aisles of meat and shakes his head. He doesn't know where to begin. Should he purchase organic free range meat and evade the guilt he feels when he supports factory farms? He is not a rich man. He cannot afford humane meat. He wonders if any meat is humane.

Anyway, he has trouble digesting meat. He feels bad enough. He feels nothing, although he drank too much coffee today.

The man wishes he never entered the store. He could have turned back in the parking lot. Now it is too late. He must purchase something. He considers purchasing a chocolate bar, but he doesn't like chocolate. He walks away from the meat and the next thing he knows, he is staring at children's cereal. The man used to like cereal. He wonders what happened. He tries to remember the last time he ate cereal. I wonder if it is normal for grownups to eat cereal with cartoon rabbits on the box, he wonders. The man cannot think about this. The light hurts his eyes.

The man will buy beer. He came to the grocery store for food, but he probably has food at home. He must have felt bored. Everything he used to love now bores him. Grocery shopping seemed like a good idea, but it was a bad idea. His ideas get worse every day.

He finds the beer section. The choices overwhelm him. Buying beer no longer seems like a good idea. He sets his grocery basket on the tile and turns to leave. It's a wonder he ever left the house.

As the automatic doors slide open, he remembers that people love him. He considers phoning some of these people, but he doesn't. Calling people takes energy and he has been tired for so long he doesn't care anymore.

The man sits at the bus stop. He will go home and lie in bed. He might be ill. If he isn't ill, he might become so. One should never take a potential illness lightly.

The bus never arrives. The man sits there for longer than he knows. It gets dark and he debates walking home. The walk really is a short one.

The sun comes up.

The man must have fallen asleep. He should call work and tell them he is sick. No, he won't call. They've probably fired him anyway. He doubts whether he ever did a satisfactory thing in his life. It seems strange to him that no bus should ever arrive and that no one else waits at this stop. Everyone must know the awful truth of it. The man curses himself for being out of the loop.

It gets dark again and he curses himself. Get with it, he says. You goddamn failure.

The grocery store closes. He wonders why he bothered or what he came for in the first place. It must be nothing good. Why else should he forget? As the temperature drops, the man crosses his arms and shivers. He tries to remember how it feels to be cold. He worries about the sickness that has threatened to consume him for so long, and the people who love him. They must be worried by now. The man laughs. His own humor creeps up on him at times. The people who love him must be worried.

A
Scorpion Town
in California

The jacket rode into town on its man. "Stay right here," the jacket said, "this is a scorpion town and men aren't welcome by scorpions."

Sliding off the man's sweaty body, the jacket told its man one last time to stay out of trouble and then slink-slithered into town.

It saw no scorpions. The jacket figured that scorpions either hated the ticklish twittering their souls made when exposed to the outer world or they were just dreaming.

It tried the saloon. There must always be a scorpion in a saloon, it thought.

All the booths and barstools stood around shuffling their feet, waiting for arachnid masters. A man on the other side of the counter slouched over a wooden crate. The jacket wondered if this man had frightened away the scorpions. He had never heard of men frightening scorpions but an old wickerwham once told him that anything was possible in California scorpion towns.

When the man opened his eyes, his skeleton leaped over the bar, blindfolded himself with the jacket, and dashed through the saloon's double doors. The jacket whipped in the wind like

47

a bullfighter's bandana hurtling through outer space.

The next day, it rained shoe polish, lobster claws, and scribbled notes that all said, "Everyone has abandoned themselves."

On the far end of a scorpion town in California, a man waits for his skeleton.

BROOM PEOPLE

I notice the girl when I come home from The Know. Until tonight, I had not left the house since Tully left. I decided to go out to the bar where we'd had our first date. Now this girl sits beside the shoebox in the bottom drawer of the dresser in my closet. Her flesh is petrified and the color of maple syrup, as if she has lived on this planet since the age of dinosaurs. Her hair is stiff straw. I ask her, "Who the hell are you? What are you doing here?"

The shoebox holds my revolver. She looks so tiny beside the box.

"I am a broom," she says, her voice a whistling kettle. "I have come to clean the cobwebs."

"Okay," I say.

I look around the bedroom. Pizza boxes and beer bottles lie scattered on the nightstand, the floor, and even the unmade bed. You can order anything online these days and have it shipped right to your door. Maybe company will be good for me, even if it's not human company. "Sure, you can clean, but how'd you get in here?"

The broom girl raises her arms. "Pick me up," she says. Her pupils twitch inside her amber eyeballs like flies. "Pick me up. I don't like guns. Why do you keep a gun in your house?"

I bend over. The last few beers I guzzled at the bar slosh to my head. Dizziness and nausea make a carousel of my brain. I nearly fall over.

"Don't squash me," the broom girl says.

I balance myself against the top of the dresser and take her in my right hand. "I think you're too short to reach the cobwebs," I say. "But if you could sweep away these boxes and bottles and maybe the dishes in the sink, I'd be grateful."

She stands in my palm, arms crossed. A frown splits her face in two. "I'm not your housekeeper."

I shrug. "So you're just a cobweb cleaner?"

The broom girl sighs. "I'd like it better if you shut up."

Same words Tully always said.

"I can shut up. I can shut up for a week, a month, a year," I say, like always.

"Better make it infinity. Now lie down on the floor and cross your arms like a dead person."

I lie down on the floor and cross my arms like a dead person. I don't know what else to do.

"Stick out your tongue."

I stick out my tongue. Between the Pizza Hut box beneath my head and the soupy fog inside me, lying here and taking orders feels comforting.

The broom girl climbs onto my stomach, employing my jacket as a ladder. She treads up my chest, across my neck, pulls herself onto my chin, and wraps her arms around my tongue. I freeze, suddenly nervous and realizing what a crazy situation I've gotten myself into.

"Calm down. This will only hurt if you let it."

The broom girl twists. She wrenches my tongue right out of my mouth. I bolt up, achingly sober. I spit blood. Hunched over. Choking. Helpless.

Behind and below me, the broom girl says, "You didn't have to let it hurt. You're stronger than this."

I wipe my mouth. My right hand comes away looking like a butchered five-legged pig. I go to the closet and grab my revolver. I spin around. The broom girl kneels on the floor and massages my severed tongue. It's the same size as the broom girl.

I aim the gun at her, arms trembling. My brain feels like it'll pop out of my head any moment. I lower the weapon. I want the broom girl dead, but I would hate to shoot my tongue. There might still exist a possibility of reconnection.

I toss the revolver onto the bed.

The broom girl kneads her fists into my tongue. She batters it into a pulpy, lifeless hunk. Is this painful to my tongue? Have the nerves and taste buds died, or does it feel the same pain as me?

Stop, I try to say. A red bubble pops on my lips. No words come out.

The sole lamp illuminating the room dances and swerves. The lamp hisses and emits a stink of human. A certain human. Tullis. Tully.

Too lightheaded to stand, I collapse. Pizza boxes pad my fall, but my knee cracks against a beer bottle. The minor pain alleviates a little of everything else that's killing me. But not enough. Nothing will ever be enough.

I crawl over to the broom girl. Tiny hands and feet jut out of my tongue. The broom girl sculpts a head out of the tip. She impresses a mouth, chews two holes for eye sockets. She spits the excess flesh into her hands and shapes a crooked nose.

I lean over her, breathing hard. The blood flowing down my face must be heavy as rain to her.

"You're blocking my light," she says.

I lean closer. I want to ask about the cobwebs. I want to shout, *If you came to sweep away the cobwebs, tell me what you're doing. Explain yourself. Explain the cobwebs. You can't, you little bitch. You can't explain cobwebs. You can't even explain yourself.*

She pauses and looks coldly at me, her pupils sad and dilated. "You're blocking my light," she says. "Let me finish what I came to do."

I slump down on my side, less than a foot away from her. I start to cry. Her busy hands blur into my tongue like two people making love in a room fractured by their hate for one another. I wipe my eyes until they burn and tell myself the broom girl is right. I am stronger than this.

"Are you feeling better? Now pay attention," she says.

I inhale as much air as possible, air mixed with blood, and look at what she's done.

Standing beside the broom girl, my tongue waves at me. They are holding hands. Only, my tongue is a miniature replica of me. "I forgot to bring some eyes," the broom girl says, "but hair and skin and nails will start to grow soon. You'll be back to normal in no time. Let's start at ground zero."

No, no, no. I shake my head.

"Why are you depressed? It's only winter," she says to the tongue version of me. I guess I can no longer lay any claim to it.

The tongue clears its throat. "Nothing of the cold or rain. Being away from you. That's what kills me."

The broom girl sighs. "We need our time apart. Spending every second of every day together is unhealthy. We've gotten too intense too quickly. I need some space."

"Like outer space?" the tongue says, in the same sarcastic tone I used when uttering the same line to Tully months ago.

"Forget it," the broom girl says, walking away.

The tongue points a meaty finger at her. "You're treating the death of our love like it's the fall of a fascist dictator. Have the past eight months really been so bad?"

"Yes, yes, because that's how it feels." The broom girl turns around. "You're so needy, so demanding. And whenever I try talking anything out, you turn my feelings into a farce, and then you get paranoid. You're so full of yourself, and you take nothing seriously."

"Why wouldn't I take *nothing* seriously?"

The broom girl throws up her arms, victorious. "That's

exactly what I mean. I won't fall for it anymore." She turns to walk away.

The tongue cartwheels after her, laughing maniacally, pushing me beyond my limit of tolerance.

I outstretch my arm and scoop up the tongue in my left hand, the broom girl in my right. I shake my head disapprovingly at both of them. I want to tell them they must go their separate ways.

The broom girl smiles at me. We lock eyes for a long time.

"Look," she says. "You're sprouting hair."

The tongue has grown a full head of stiff, long hair. A broom head. My miniature is a tongue-broom man.

"You've learned so quick," the broom girl says. "I knew you were strong, and you found that strength in yourself. Now you can sweep up your own cobwebs whenever they build up."

Panic clutches at my heart. She can't go. I can't let her. She's done so much for me. I'll go back to being miserable if she leaves now. Maybe a little later, after my tongue returns to its proper place.

She recognizes my horror, and smiles. I catch my reflection in her amber eyes. "Do you want me to stay with you?" she says.

I nod.

The tongue-broom man bites my hand. I drop him and he scurries beneath the bed. "No need to worry about him," the broom girl tells me. "He's just a bunch of cobwebs."

"We can be together forever. Let me show you how."

She skips over to edge of the bed and reaches for a blanket hanging off the edge. She fails to grab hold. I'm unsure whether to help or sit back and watch. So I sit back and watch.

The tongue-broom man reappears. He bows like a gentleman. "Let me help you," he says to her. He urges me over, then gestures for me to lower my head. "Help us onto the bed," he says. "Do right by both of us, the good and the bad, because we're the same at heart."

I turn my hands palm-up on the floor. The broom girl and tongue-broom man each step into one. I raise them to the bed. They scurry toward the revolver. The broom girl tilts her head to one side and frowns. "I don't like guns. Why do you keep a gun in your house?"

"Sometimes for protection, sometimes for peace of mind. Sometimes when the ones you love turn your world upside down, you want to take them with you," the tongue-broom man says.

The broom girl turns to me. "Is this true for you also?"

I try to open my mouth and find that blood has sealed it shut. Incapable of speech, I'm clueless as to how to respond.

"Nevermind," she says. "I want to play a game. Pick up the gun and point it at my head. Let's pretend this has never happened before. Everything is make-believe."

I don't want her to leave, so I pick up the revolver and point it at her head.

"Ready," she says.

I will do as she says, for she has done so much to save me.

"Aim," she says.

My heart set to explode.

"Remember this is all a game," she says. "And fire!"

I squeeze the trigger. Click, an empty chamber.

"Fire!" the broom girl screams.

The tongue-broom man joins her in a duet of "*Fire! Fire! Fire!*"

I lower the gun. I don't need the broom girl anymore, and she never needed me. I raise the gun again and find the strength inside myself, a clumsy human strength, and fire at the tongue-broom man, my miniature. There is more than a chamber click this time. What happens is louder and emptier than a cobweb, and unspeakable.

LAZY FASCIST

I grow a mustache. It is a fascist mustache. The fascist mustache conquers my face. I am sad because my face is oppressed. The mustache turns my nose into a vodka distillery. My fascist mustache spends most of its time in the distillery. It even sleeps in there. My mustache is a lazy drunkard, but whenever I try sneezing it out or brushing it off my face, the mustache stabs me with its well-groomed, razor-toothed hairs. "I will squash your rebellion," the mustache says, so I don't rebel. I think to myself, *God damn you, mustache. God damn you.*

The mustache says I cannot wash my face anymore. It is popping zits and distilling the pus into vodka at an alarming rate. The mustache needs more pimples and that just won't happen if I'm taking care of my complexion. When the mustache is not making vodka or drinking vodka, it goes on parade. It marches from my chin all the way up to the crown of my shaved head. The mustache says, "Someday the whole world will be mine!"

The mustache never tries to expand its empire. It is too lazy to put any effort into being a good fascist. It drinks vodka, holds parades, combs its hairs, and makes empty threats to me and my body.

One day, guerilla scissors invade my feet. My mustache is

too lazy to fend off the radicals. I am quickly cut apart. When the scissors have destroyed me up to my heart, the lazy fascist leaps off my face, plunging to a cowardly, self-inflicted death. I open my mouth to cry my first free words since I grew a mustache, but my vocal cords are already in tatters. After my face is liberated by the army of scissors, the scissors lay siege on the nasal distillery. They hold a toast to Victory and the sovereign, crippled, unrecognizable, totally fucked nation of Me.

The drunken scissors make snow angels in a pile of my guts and bones and call it a treatise on the means of production. Beneath my guts and bones lies the squishy hollow of my brain. In the squishy hollow of my brain, the hairs of a baby mustache goosestep in blood-shaped lines.

THE
DRESSING BOOTH

On the day James Timmerman could no longer face himself, he awoke naked in a dressing booth. He was musty and damp and his head ached.

A gray suit hung from the hook on the back of the door, so he took the pants and suit jacket off the hook and put them on. No other articles had been provided.

James reached for the door handle.

He hesitated.

It was not so much the contact between his hand and the door handle that he dreaded, but how he felt as if he were viewing himself from somewhere else as he reached for the door. James sat on the dressing room bench to contemplate this crisis.

He sat for many days.

A week passed.

"I will have to break the mirror if I want to leave," he said. "I can waste no more time."

He had grown old, as if each day were a full decade.

He stood up and punched the dressing room mirror. He punched it again and again. He kicked it. He punched it until his fingers broke.

His legs collapsed and he fell and hit the wall. In his week of thinking and aging, he had lost the strength to smash the dressing room mirror using his fists or feet.

His vision turned fuzzy. He was out of breath.

When he finally caught his breath, he struggled to his feet and tried lifting the dressing room bench to throw it into the mirror.

He failed miserably. The bench would not budge. He took a deep breath and exhaled, "Remain calm, James, remain calm. You've missed the simplest solution."

He reached for the door handle, trying not to fear it.

He twisted the handle, but the door was locked from the outside.

"Please," he cried. "Let me return to my life."

"This is your life," a voice said.

He did not know where it came from. He did not know who it was.

"Who are you? I demand answers," he said.

He received no reply.

He banged on the door until the cuts on his fingers split open again and his hands folded into black and blue claws.

Exasperated, he took off his suit and threw himself against the walls of his holding cell.

And accidentally glimpsed his naked, skeletal body in the mirror. He shuddered and turned away, and crumpled into a ball on the dressing bench. He was so pale and featureless. A weakling. A faceless blob.

"James, look in the mirror," the voice said, from just the other side of the door.

"Why should I?" he said, face buried in his hands.

"Look in the mirror and I'll let you out."

James raised his head and forced himself to look in the mirror. The thing in the mirror no longer had a nose or mouth, only eyes. All he had were eyes.

The unblinking mirror face nodded. James reached out

to touch it, his fingers trembling, but every time his hand approached the mirror he felt cold all over. The mirror possessed no resemblance to him at all. Breaking it would be a futile waste. Even looking at it was a futile waste. He needed to blind himself, to gouge out his own eyes and lose sight forever. *It is better to be blind*, he thought, *than to be like that man.*

"Will you free me now?" he said. "Let me go!"

The buzzing electric lights running along the ceiling died and the dressing room went dark.

He heard the pitter-patter of footsteps. He fumbled around for the gray suit on the floor and called out. "Show me who you are. I know you're there. Show your face, goddamn you."

The footsteps approached his dressing booth. He wondered if the footsteps belonged to the voice. He wondered if other dressing booths existed in the dressing room, or if his was the only one.

The footsteps stopped on the other side of the door. He heard breathing. He reached for the handle but jerked away. Whoever stood on the other side, they would have to open it themselves.

They knocked.

"Whoever it is, go away," he said, out of old habit.

He was so startled by the knocking that he wanted to crawl inside the mirror just to escape that door, and all others, forever.

"Death will catch up to you," said the voice.

James felt uncertain earlier. Now he decided. It was not a human voice. It could not be human. It was better if it was not.

"Just go the hell away, will you?" James said.

Footsteps receded.

"What a rotten scheme," he muttered. "I don't belong here."

"Are we having fun now?" said the voice, from right inside the dressing booth.

"Who are you? How many of you are there?" he said.

The footsteps were gone, but the owner of the voice should've been standing right next to James. He groped around in the dark and found no one. Pangs, sharp as the appendicitis he once endured, pierced his side. As he rolled about on the floor, catching brief, blackened flashes of himself in the mirror, a red light flickered above the dressing booth.

"Did you do something bad, James? Is that why you could no longer face yourself?" said the voice. The red light flickered in sync with the voice. The walls of the dressing booth rattled.

"Who are you?" James said, between gritted teeth.

"This is a quiet life you're leading, cooped up like a factory chicken. Do you like your dressing booth? Did I pick a good one for you? Do you like your gray suit? Are you having fun? Why don't you come out for sunshine? You remember sunshine, don't you? Or can you not face it?

"Why could you no longer face yourself? Don't answer. I know. Do you know, James? Do you know why you came here? Do you know who I am?"

"Go away, goddamn you!"

"That's the spirit. Goodbye, James. Enjoy your dressing booth."

A door opened and shut. The red light dissipated and the overhead lights turned back on. James rubbed his eyes. The piercing in his side softened to a dull throb. He felt forsaken, but by whom or what he did not know.

Days and weeks passed.

The voice did not visit. It had spoken its part, James knew.

He sat on the bench, gazing up into the fluorescent lights until sunspots pixilated his scope. It was a resigned way of life. He felt detached from himself and even enjoyed his detachment. During this period, he did not move at all. He just stared at the lights.

A year or more went by, until one day he folded his hands in his lap. Startled, he tore his vision from the lights and looked at his hands. He rolled up the sleeves of his jacket and felt his wrists. Although his vision was fractured, he still saw that his skin had flaked away. He was nothing more than a skeleton. "I can waste no more time," he said, finally knowing what had to be done.

James turned his head slowly. His neck crackled and popped. He looked in the mirror, voluntarily now, and smiled—

PERSONAL SAVIORS

You're sitting cross-legged in a field, thinking you're finally ready to trust the chemists.

What's the worst that could happen? After all, they're offering to pay the mortgage on all those fried serotonin receptors. And even if they've mutated six billion people into brain-eating atrocities, they spared *your* ass, right?

Okay, you'll give it a shot.

Whoa.

The moment you decide you'll go with their program, a fishy manta hand reaches down from heaven and sets a pill and a slip of paper at your feet. You wipe the pill on your jeans to get some of the dirt off and unfold the paper.

According to the slip, the pill in your hand is a tryptamine compound, plus two methyl groups. The directions say, "Crush it up and smoke it." And because you trust the fish-faced chemists in the sky, you crush the pill and pack your pipe.

Hold it.

Animals scream beyond the foxtails. At least you think they're animals. Maybe some goats getting munched by the dead. You set the pipe beside you. The chemist who gave you the pill stares down at you from above the marine layer. The chemist is making this noise. The chemist is screaming at you, pissed that you're not smoking its magic pill. For days you thought they didn't speak, like hardcore silent monks.

Now they are screaming. Projecting their goat cries into the field around you, howling in the wind and the grain. You marvel that the chemists sound so nasally, seeing how they look like stuntmen in bad manta ray costumes.

You're ready this time. So many dead receptors in your skull and even more dead people walking the planet, of course you'll trust the chemists. After all, they're gods or something. You suppress the nagging worry that you might be wrong, but the alternative is that much worse. Getting your brains munched by shambling death machines would be a lousy way to die.

You raise the pipe to your lips and torch the crushed pill.

Inhale. Hold it in. Breathe out.

Two hits later, a bundle of white snakes falls from the sky. All knotted together, the snakes form a ladder leading to heaven. A chemist holds the top of the ladder and waves a manta hand. It wants you to climb.

Now the goat cries sound more like hissing roaches. You wonder if they always sounded this way, if you heard wrong before. It's true, you've lost a lot of the best things in your life through simple misunderstandings, like when you and Leslie broke up last week, the day before the chemists appeared in the sky, and she said—

Hold it.

Not the time, man. Get her out of your head. You've got to trust the chemists. Christ, with what they did to Leslie and everyone else on the planet, how *could* you trust them? But you've got to. You've got to find out why they offered to fix your head. Maybe you're so damaged that making you into a dead thing is impossible. Whatever the reason, they're sparing your ass. Take advantage of that.

The insect noises vibrate the air around you. Calm down, breathe. If the chemists want you to climb their snake ladder, you damn well better climb it.

You step onto the ladder. Remember, take it one step at a

time and don't look down. Above, the chemist who gave you the pill nods and holds the ladder steady. Yes, you think, almost free of this wasteland.

Climb.

Twenty feet up.

Forty.

You must be one hundred feet high now. They'll take you in, you tell yourself. They'll fix your transmitters, your receptors. They won't screw with you. They won't fuck you over like they did everyone else, all the people now wandering the planet as mindless skull-biters. You will be enlightened to the cause of the world's demise, you tell yourself.

You're halfway to the top when you look down and it just might be the worst mistake in your short, miserable life.

Thousands of the dead scuttle in the field. You force yourself to look away.

You always forget how awful their appearance really is. They're nothing like the zombies of Romero or Fulci. Hell, you wouldn't even call them zombies. Hundreds of legs, dark glassy flesh, eyeless . . . you call them centipeople. A brand new species. Manufactured by the chemists in the sky, your personal saviors.

The centipeople grab for the ladder and you scramble upward. No turning back now. The higher you climb, the more your head throbs.

You hope it's only another fifty feet to the top, but you could be wrong. Your skull pounds so bad you're afraid it'll burst. You fix your eyes on the chemist above and force yourself not to look down again. Remember to breathe and keep your foothold.

Breathe breathe breathe.

The chemist grabs your arm and pulls you into Heaven.

And you realize your mistake.

Being a centiperson does not equal being undead. Centipeople equal larvae. This notion pops into your head as blue-gray manta hands strip off your rags and carry you up a staircase of clouds. The chemists must be telepathically charged, which explains how they led you to the field in the first place and provided the pill the moment you decided to submit to them. It also means you're fucked.

At the top of the stairs, four chemists hold a giant wooden sun. The chemist that helped you into heaven opens its fishy slit of a mouth and says, "The sun cannot be the sun. It can only represent the sun."

The chemists holding the wooden sun tilt it downward. The one holding you slides your body onto this so-called representation. You struggle but they hold you down.

You vomit blood as they nail you to the wooden sun.

Nobody wants to save you. You've been taken for a fool. Your head explodes. A million gallons of your blood and brain matter leak down the staircase and out of Heaven, onto the dead below. Cleansed in your sacrifice, they rejoice. The dead are ready to hatch. Your teeth fall from heaven and scatter in the field, trampled by the million-footed dead. Your teeth howl in the wind and the grain, and they join the forsaken cries of teeth belonging to other saviors across the planet.

You wait for rebirth.

EMBRYO TREE FOR ANDROID

Inside the first room of the cosmos, a shadow emerged from a patch of blue-black fungus on the door. It sprouted limbs and genitals, eye sockets and mouths. After the first in a series of grand mal seizures, the shadow separated into two shadows. The two shadows mated. Together, they gave birth to Android.

"What will we feed it?" said the first shadow.

"The door fungus won't last," said the second.

And so the shadows collected the white beetles that nested in the fluffy darkness of their bellies. They crushed up the insects and ground them into the door fungus. Dissatisfied, they mated once more, crushing up the new birth-creature's skull and using its red blood as a sort of glue that held the beetles and the fungus together.

"This is what we feed Android," said the first shadow.

"Android will be pleased," said the second.

They scuttled to the corner of the room where Android was dreaming. "We have brought you food," said the shadows.

Android did not move.

"It must be dreaming new rooms," said the first shadow.

"But it must be hungry," said the second shadow.

The first insisted that Android must be hungry, so they tried harder to wake their crustaceous metal child, but Android still failed to wake. The first shadow crawled into Android's mouth and inspected the black box in Android's chest. The box was silent. The shadow returned to the room through the Android's mouth and said, "Android is dead."

The shadows tried grieving for the loss of their child, but since each of them was no longer a whole shadow, they did not possess the capacity to feel sadness.

"What will we do about this?" said the first shadow.

"It is wrong not to grieve now that our firstborn is dead," said the second shadow. "Now there will always be something to grieve for. Let us commit ourselves to suffering."

The first shadow agreed, and so they set about planning their descent into perpetual unhappiness.

Since the shadows had originally been one, it seemed appropriate to create a new creature to be their double so that each shadow-half could be completed with this new, other half, and then together they could suffer. They called the new beings Human, a word that had come to the shadows in a jointly experienced death dream.

"How should we create Human?" said the second shadow.

"Human should be dreamed," said the first, "because Android died dreaming."

The shadows wrapped themselves around each other and closed their eyes. They waited to dream of Human, but the dream never came. Instead, they dreamed of mushrooms sprouting from a black monolith. The slimy white mushrooms decayed on the black stone almost as fast as they appeared. The fallen mushrooms floated around the base of the monolith, wilting into little skeletons that resembled what would eventually be known as Human.

They approached the black monolith.

"How should we create Human?" said the second shadow.

"By eating the mushrooms," said the first.

They grabbed at the mushrooms, shoving only the most

decayed specimens in their mouths to increase their personal suffering, but shortly after their miserable feast began, a spike-mouthed gray worm crawled out of the monolith and said, "You are not welcome here."

The shadows suddenly found themselves in a black desert with no sky above.

"There is no more room for us in the universe," said the second shadow.

"At least we have dreamed of Embryo Tree," said the first.

"We have nothing but this desert, now," said the second.

"But our sacrifice will bring Human into being," the first shadow said.

"I wish we could see it."

"Maybe Android can see it."

"Android sees nothing."

"We failed," said the first shadow. "We have given up our room in the cosmos. Now the room houses Human, but Human is a mirror to us. Without us, Human reflects dead images."

"No," said the second. "Android is still in that room."

"Android is dead."

"So the humans will reflect dead Android."

After a while, the black desert grew darker and the first shadow said, "Do you think our suffering was worth it?"

"I expected something else."

"Regret is not much to expect."

Each shadow, beginning to confuse itself with the other shadow, laid down in the dry sand of the black desert with no sky. They snuggled close, and quickly lost their bodies in each other. Together, in umbra sadness, they regretted giving birth.

HOW TO LIVE FOREVER

Time had frozen in southern California. People got stuck in Los Angeles traffic for sixty years. While trying to create a black hole on the side of Highway 101, Charles Bender had glued Time to his cardboard hands. He was a clumsy scientist. It took six earth decades to unstick Time. The flesh peeled off of his hands, so when Time kicked into gear again, Charles was transported to the center northbound lane of Highway 101. Los Angeles traffic turned into a deadly board game where nobody died. Cars ate their drivers and digested them into fuel. Officers on motorcycles rode around as mad-robotic gargoyles. The freeways lifted up and licked the sky like concrete tongues. Charles the Scientist received the worst of the lot. Now he was nothing more than a giant rubber hand.

Charles froggered across Highway 101 on his four fingers. A semi with the face of a dragon belched fire and scorched the metal hairs on his thumb-head. Charles went blind and fell onto a cactus beside the road. The spines of the cactus pierced his fingertips and side. His face melted. Nobody died anymore, so he laid there and listened to the world play out in fast forward. He cursed his miserable predicament and wondered what went wrong with his experiment. He had always dreamed of living forever, but not like this. This was not what he envisioned when he schemed up a plan to live forever.

The machine creatures honked and screeched. It sounded like they were enjoying the new world. Charles Bender sighed. He would be stuck here for a long time.

Some while later, an owl-shaped helicopter swooped down and took Charles in its beak. The evil noise of traffic faded. Charles Bender's hollow stomach churned as he rose higher into the air. *Thank God I am saved*, he thought. A deflated smile appeared on his melted face. But the helicopter was without a pilot and had scooped him up by mere chance. It dropped Charles when it reached the upper layer of smog, favoring a winged otter over his rubber body. Charles fell. He landed in a bush beside the highway. He laughed now, for the tyranny of life was such a joyous, mysterious thing.

A semi spit flames, lighting Charles and the bush on fire.

Somewhere in Hollywood, a black hole checked into a motel.

Tea for a Mysterious Creature

A mysterious creature follows me home. I want to call it a raccoon but it looks nothing like a raccoon. Its fur is blue, its face round as a dinner plate. I turn and tell it, "Creature, go away."

It gapes like a salmon. I open the front door and walk inside, remembering last night's salmon dinner.

Teresa dumped me last night. She broke the news right after we ate peach cobbler. In my belly, the salmon we baked still feels worse than rat poison.

A cardboard box sits on the kitchen counter. The box is full of Teresa's kitchen knickknacks. The shelves are bare. I realize how little I own.

The creature opens the door. It hops onto the counter and heats the kettle and says, "Tea."

"I'm sorry," I say. "The tea's been packed. It's on its way out."

The creature, which now looks like a bird with hands, claps its hands and grumbles.

I have never been followed home by a mysterious creature, but I'm sad and lonely and feverish in heartbreak and salmon sickness. "Alright, I'll get you tea. But let me warn you, this will upset Teresa. Wild animals frighten her. If she catches you drinking tea, she might lose it."

I pull back the flaps of the cardboard box and dig through canned foods, spice bottles, a dual can opener/spatula, shot glasses, ketchup and mustard packets, silverware, measuring cups, and other painfully familiar items that are on their way out. Piled in the box, they appear alien. Their haphazard grouping makes it evident that Teresa, a self-admitted neat freak, packed them in a hurry.

I find tea bags at the bottom of the box. "Hope you don't mind cheap green," I say, wondering if I should be talking to this creature. Who knows how much it understands? For all I know, some very lonesome widow taught it how to ask for tea.

The creature holds out an open palm. I place the tea bags in its feathered palm.

I decide to test this creature. After all, it followed me home and asked for tea. I ask, "Do you understand the things people say?"

It nods and sticks out its tongue. The kettle whistles. The creature turns off the stove and dangles the tea bags by their strings. "Mugs," it says.

I fish a mug out of the box and hand it to the creature. It drops a bag into the mug and holds up three fingers. "Mugs," it says.

"No, I don't think so," I say. "One mug is enough."

The creature sighs. It picks up the kettle and concentrates on pouring the steaming water. After it fills the mug, it floats off the counter, sets its bird feet down on the linoleum, and waddles to the kitchen table. It sits on a chair like a regular guest.

Since many months will pass before my life feels whole again, and without any friends to call on, I figure wasting a few minutes in idle conversation might be good for me. I might have no one to talk to for a long time.

I sit down at the table and clasp my hands. "So what do you do?" I say.

The creature blows on the tea. It sniffs at the rising steam and ignores the question, stifling my small hope for conversation. "I guess you don't understand anything but tea," I say.

It blinks at the ceiling and says, "Follow."

"Follow?"

"What I do is follow," it says.

"Oh, so you do understand."

The creature sips at the tea. "I understand a lot of things. Understanding is easy when you follow things around for long enough. You, for instance."

I sit up in the chair and say, "You've been following me?" The creature licks the rim of the mug. "One evening by a river, I saw you with a woman. You both looked so unhappy. I wanted to understand why you stayed together if you made each other miserable."

So the little blue snoop has been spying on Teresa and I. "You followed us? I should kick your ass," I say, trying my best to intimidate the creature.

"It was open knowledge to anyone who saw you. The difference is that I cannot ignore these things. I must understand them."

"So you followed me."

"So I followed you."

"Well, she left me. Now I'm twice as miserable. Does that satisfy you? Do you understand that sometimes it's worse to be alone than with the people who torment you?"

"I am always alone. I never feel dissatisfied or miserable. Nothing torments me." The creature slides the mug toward me. "Drink up."

"You must be a special case," I say, wiping my sweater sleeve along the mug's rim. "Anyway, you're not human. You don't know what it means to feel."

"Oh, but I feel."

The tea has gone lukewarm. I gulp it down. I halfheartedly hope to catch an alien virus from this creature, which now resembles a warty toad. I marvel that I could have been so blind and wrong to mistake it for a raccoon or a bird.

Right then Teresa walks in the door. She stops cold and says, "What the hell is that?" She says this in a stern but gentle voice.

"It's a mysterious creature," I say.

"Whatever," she says, and leaves the kitchen.

The creature climbs down from its chair and follows her. "Ma'am," it says, "mam, may I speak with you for a minute? Just one minute of your time, mam."

"What kind of sick joke is this, Gary?" Teresa yells.

"It followed me home. Is it such a crime for mysterious creatures to follow people home?" Maybe it's a symptom of the breakup, but I want to defend this creature, even if I'm furious at it for following me and want nothing more to do with it. Maybe I'm only desperate and clinging to what's gone.

Teresa slams the bedroom door. I hear the creature pawing at the hinges. It knocks and calls out in a soft voice, "Ma'am, this man you call Gary says he's twice as miserable without you. Is this true for you too? Are you twice as miserable without him?"

Teresa yells and stomps across the bedroom. I walk into the living room just as she opens the bedroom door a crack and says, "That man I call Gary is an asshole. You're a fool to think I'm worse off without him."

"I know how miserable he made you," the little bastard says. "I assumed nothing, ma'am. I merely asked a question."

"Stop asking!" Teresa says. She cranes her neck around door and glares at me. "Gary, take your pet and get out of here. I'll be gone in an hour."

She slams the door.

I sit on the couch and hang my head and cry. The creature pads over to me. It hops onto the couch and rests a hand on my shoulder. It sits close to me, wheezing. "Why do you cry?" it says.

"Leave me alone," I say. "Go away. Stop bothering me."

I shake my head and sob.

From the bedroom, Teresa yells, "Which copy of The Metamorphosis is mine?"

"Yours is the dog-eared one," I respond, "unless you bent the pages of mine as well."

A few minutes go by, then Teresa yells again. "What did you do with my Astral Weeks LP?"

I try to say it's in the den, still on the record player from when I played it on repeat last night. I'm too ashamed to respond. The only other time Teresa saw me cry was at my father's funeral. "I wanted so bad to make things right," I say.

"Do you think you failed?" the creature says.

"I know I failed. Why else would I feel so terrible?"

"You enjoy being miserable, don't you?" it says.

I raise my head. Through my tears, the creature looks like a blob of Jello.

"I gave you tea," I say, wiping my eyes. "Can't you go?"

"I came for more than tea," the creature says.

"So you said."

The ugly thing nods. "Tell me why you enjoy being miserable."

In the bedroom, something crashes to the floor. It must be the bookshelf. That's the heaviest piece of furniture in there. Startled by the crash, the creature lets go of my shoulder and covers its eyes. It burrows between two cushions and cowers there, whimpering like a chastised puppy.

I laugh a little at this. "You've got no idea how hard it is to love and be loved and struggle to find joy in the shit people put each other through," I say. "I can't reject the awful parts. Even when miserable, I'm overjoyed by it all." The hypocrisy of saying this as I'm crying and feeling like death doesn't evade me. After the crash, Teresa has been silent. I'm starting to wonder if she's alright in there. Beside me, the creature peeks a red eye between two pale fingers.

I get up from the couch and move toward the bedroom door.

I reach for the handle, then turn back to face the mysterious creature. It nods and waves me on, once again resembling a raccoon.

I open the door. Books are scattered across the floor. Teresa lies on the bed. She cries into a pillow. My Batman pillowcase. She took all the other pillows. I clear my throat, choking down sobs, and say, "Is there anything I can do?"

She buries her face deeper into the pillow. I hope the bookshelf didn't fall on her hand or something. Maybe it hit her head. Maybe she needs to go to the hospital. She mumbles into the pillow.

"I can't hear you," I say. "If you need help, you've got to speak clearly."

She lifts her head and stares at me, eyeliner streaking her cheeks. "I can't leave," she says. "I tried to leave and I can't."

I slump onto the bed beside her. The bedroom door is still open a crack. I want to put my arms around her but worry what she might say. I fear that she would recoil from me, like she did all week, even before she told me last night that she and Rob had been—

"What about last night?" I say.

She touches my thigh and says, "There's got to be some way we can make this work."

"That's not what you said last night," I say, crying again. "That's the total opposite of what you said."

Teresa and I lean in to each other and embrace, our wet cheeks touching. We jump apart when the front door slams shut. The mysterious creature must be gone. I brush tears from her cheeks as she pulls me close to her.

We lie down.

It seems like forever passes before either of us says a word.

We crawl out of bed.

After we repair the bookshelf, we go into the kitchen. I

fill the kettle with water and turn on the stove. Teresa sits at the kitchen table. I look out the window in the door, so badly wanting to step outside and smoke a cigarette on the porch. Instead, I sit across from Teresa at the table.

"What should I tell Rob?" she says.

I shrug.

"You've known him longer," she says.

Our hands are locked together on the table.

When the kettle whistles, I get up and turn it off. I look for the box of cheap green tea but it is not on the counter and not in the box of kitchen supplies. The tea is simply gone.

I move from the stove to the door. I lean my face into the window and scan the yard. To the right of the chestnut tree, I spot the mysterious creature. It sits on the tire swing, holding the box of green tea in its lap.

"What's wrong?" Teresa says.

I open the door and step onto the porch. As I cross the overgrown summer lawn, I feel like I'm gliding. I pass some bushes overloaded with blackberries. I stop in front of the creature sitting on the tire swing. The creature resembles a bluebird now. It holds the box of tea in its beak.

"Want me to push you?" I say, pointing at the ropes of the swing.

"Tea," the mysterious creature says. The box falls from its mouth.

The creature flaps its wings and takes flight.

I pick up the fallen box. I head toward the closed door of the house. Teresa stands on the porch. She's crying into her cell phone.

I'm halfway across the lawn when she walks inside and slams the door behind her.

I stop, frozen. I don't know how long I stand there, staring at the house. I can't bring myself to go inside now. I'm worried about what that phone call means, so I turn around and retrace my steps.

The sun melts on the horizon, clinging on for dear life. The red and purple clouds, puffy like cotton candy, lose out to a breezy summer night.

Even as the dark comes, no lights turn on in the house, but I'm not ready to go inside and turn them on myself.

I sit on the tire swing and hold the box of tea in my lap.

"Tea," I say.

Belatedly, I will name it Tea.

FLOWERS

When Franz Kafka's ghost awoke, he found himself transformed in his coffin into a flower. Clawing with his petals at the coffin lid, Kafka's ghost began to sweat a glow-in-the-dark juice that stank of sulfur. "This must be my spirit leaking out," he said, and ceased clawing to preserve what remained of his soul.

"This might be Hell," he said, "but a man could truly sleep down here."

Yawning, Franz Kafka curled his petals (seven, he counted) beneath his frail, leafy belly. With no alarm clock to disturb the sleep of the dead, Kafka's now-comfortable ghost nodded off to nightmares of diamond-eyed golems eating the sky. He dreamed of insects reading the scriptures in muddy corners of the cosmos, and in those scriptures he caught muttered accusations against shapeless, yet-to-be-named insects. Among those judgments, he overheard his own name. He beheld a vision of himself as one of those nameless vermin, and of the terminal white light with which every life bloomed before consuming its own petals.

THE
DEAD MONKEY
EXHIBIT

A monkey with amputated limbs gave birth to a meat-eating plant in the monkey pen at the zoo. The monkey had a history of giving birth to meat-eating plants. The meat-eating plants the monkey gave birth to did not eat monkeys. The meat-eating plants liked eating lions. In order to eat lions, the meat-eating plants needed to lure the lions into the monkey pen. To lure the lions into the cage, the meat-eating plants amputated the limbs of monkeys and tied the limbs to ropes.

As the monkeys screamed over their missing arms and legs and other limbs, limbs without names, the monkeys dragged themselves around the cage. Their limbs hung from the ceiling like furry chandeliers strung with red crystal lights that dripped. The smell of monkey blood attracted the lions a few cages down. The lions licked the air. "Yum," they said. They unlocked the door of their cage and people screamed even though the lions did not want to hurt them. "We will not hurt you," the lions said.

The lions marched past crying children and crying mothers and crying fathers and crying people who were crying for other reasons, maybe because they came to the zoo by themselves and felt alone. The lions marched past the wombat cage and the panda bear cage until finally they stood outside the monkey cage. The meat-eating plants crouched behind rocks. They looked at each other and held their hands over their mouths to contain their laughter. Playing tricks on lions was so much fun.

The lions unlocked the door of the monkey cage and entered the cage single file. They stood on their hind legs and batted at the monkey limbs hanging from the ceiling. They took the limbs in their jaws. They ignored the screaming, bleeding monkeys. Lions were not that interested in eating real, live monkeys. That seemed inhumane. The lions did not know that monkey limbs came from real, live monkeys. If they knew, maybe they would have stopped eating monkey limbs. Maybe they would have eaten salads instead. The lions stuffed their mouths with limbs to contain their laughter. Eating monkey limbs was so much fun. The meat-eating plants nodded to each other and leaped from behind the rocks. They attacked the lions and the lions were helpless because their mouths and bellies were full of limbs. The meat-eating plants ate the lions, leaving not a bone or golden hair behind.

By now, the crying people had alerted the zookeeper. The zookeeper, who was very old, limped up to the monkey cage with a cane in one hand and a shotgun in the other. The zookeeper took aim. He squinted down the barrel of the gun, an old habit that reminded him of hunting with his father as a child. The habit was useless. He was blind in both eyes. He pulled the trigger. He shot bullets into the cage until he had killed all of the meat-eating plants and all of the screaming, bleeding monkeys.

The zookeeper sighed. He had even killed the dead lions that were inside the meat-eating plants and the dead monkey limbs that were inside the dead lions. He reached into his pocket and pulled out a sticker. The sticker pronounced, in black letters on a white background:

DEAD

The zookeeper peeled the backing off the sticker and stuck it on the sign outside the monkey cage. Now the sign outside the monkey cage read DEAD MONKEY EXHIBIT. The zookeeper rested his forehead on the bars of the monkey cage. In a moment he would return to his dark shed, but not for long. He would have to order new lions from Africa, and the monkey with amputated limbs never stayed dead. It returned to life again and again, always spreading its life to the other monkeys, and they always grew new limbs. Then the zookeeper had to limp out of his dark shed to cover up the word DEAD on the sign outside the monkey cage. Then the new lions came in from Africa and the monkey with amputated limbs gave birth to meat-eating plants. That was the routine. He hated it, but as long as the monkeys were alive and the lions were in their cages, the people did not cry.

The zookeeper limped past the crying people and returned to his dark shed. He sat on the stool in the corner and held his face in his hands.

DRAIN ANGEL

ONE

Joy Erickson did not scream when the cherub-faced earwig crawled out of the shower drain. She pursed her lips, slipped into her bathrobe, and resolved to squash the poor thing with a shampoo bottle. She did not scream, though she wanted to.

The insect grew until it was the size of an infant. It raised one mildew-sheathed arm and let out a soft wail. The other arm was tangled in an impossible knot around the grill of the drain.

Joy dropped the shampoo bottle. She bent down and reached for the sad insect baby. She stroked its cherubic face, registering a purring vibration within its scaly belly. The dark slime that coated the creature blackened the shower tiles and seeped into Joy's hands and feet. She pitied the creature and felt nauseated. Its insect mewling made her think of sick cows, but she realized that it was an angel, come to her from heaven. It had to be an angel.

She leaned against the shower wall and feared she would collapse. She wanted to scream for Bill, to have someone here beside her, but she couldn't. She just couldn't. A creature that screams like a cow, she thought, Bill and his anxiety could never face that. Joy swallowed her faintness and picked up the angel. How I found a curious husband, she thought. Her robe blossomed out across the shower tiles and the angel whimpered beneath the darkness of the cottony folds.

She walked through the master bathroom, the bedroom, and came into the hall, stopping at the top of the stairs.

"Bill, come here a moment. I want to show you something," she called. She would show him after all. Slippery as a perch, the angel squirmed in her grip. Downstairs, Bill muted the television.

"What was that, honey?" he said.

"I need to show you something," Joy said.

"But the game's on," Bill said. "There's three minutes left and if the Raiders win, they're going to the playoffs. Do you know what this could mean for history?"

Joy rolled her eyes. She pulled an old quilt from the closet at the end of the hall and wrapped up the angel. "There you are," she said, smiling down at its eyeless cricket face. "Is that better?"

"Can't this wait?" Bill yelled.

"Go ahead, Bill," she said.

Sound returned to the television. A commercial for a new pharmaceutical blared. She cradled the angel, glad that her pretty thing was wrapped up so warm and tight, forever free of the shower drain.

"We can't keep it," Bill said. He paced from one end of their room to the other. From the rip down the center of his Raiders jersey, Joy assumed history would not be made today.

"It's an angel," she said. "You can't very well throw away an angel, can you?"

"God dammit, that thing is not an angel," he said, fumbling through the top drawer of his nightstand. "Where are my pills? Oh, for chrissake, get that nasty thing out of our bed. How can you call it an angel? Where are my pills?"

"Lower your voice, Bill. It's exhausted. You don't know how hard it is to climb out of a shower drain and nearly lose an arm along the way. Your pills are downstairs."

Bill hurried toward the bedroom door in a mad dash for the staircase. "I know that anything crawling out of any drain in this house deserves to be squashed *and* exterminated. I also know that you're crazy if you believe it's an angel. No, you're crazy anyway, letting it sleep in our bed. What's come over you? Oh lord, I need my pills. Do you want one? They'll help you think like a normal person for once."

Joy stood at the top of the stairs, hands poised on her hips because she knew how that pose intimidated Bill. "Nothing can change my mind. It's an angel and I'm taking care of it. If you don't like how things are, you can sleep in the garage."

Bill stood in the doorway and swore he wouldn't come home until he'd gotten drunk and crashed into a busload of kids.

"Goodbye, Bill," Joy said. She knew this routine. "Be safe and don't scratch the new car." She recalled the lipstick stains recently appearing on his collars. "And if you do crash the car, at least wear a clean shirt. That way I won't be scandalized."

"Scandalized?" he said. "Scandalized? I'm living in a fucking freak show! My life is a nightmare."

"You're sterile."

"What's that?" Bill scoffed.

"It's natural for me to want a child, and you're sterile. I've found my own child now."

"That thing's been in our home for hardly an hour and do you see what it's done to you? Oh, fuck it. You can keep the critter. Next week you'll want a new puppy, and the week after—"

"Yes, Bill. I want a new puppy."

He slammed the door. Joy thought this would be oh so funny in a doll's house, but it was not funny now. But everything is fine, she thought, everything will work out in the end. Even failed marriages worked out in the end. What are door slams and car crashes? Anyway, good riddance to Bill. What dreadful influence he would have on the angel! Without him, she was better off.

The guest bedroom would have to do. What other room in the house possibly possessed the right character to raise her angel? She laughed. Oh my, maybe you are getting a bit crazy, talking about *your* angel, she thought. In a sense, it did belong to her. It belonged to her and no one else. She found the angel, accepted the task of raising it, and thereby gained the right to call it her baby. Joy never considered herself religious in the church-going sense, but she felt positive that she would be rewarded for her sacrifices in raising this angel. She wanted to call her mother and inquire about raising infants, but the old woman might not understand the dynamics of this complex parental situation.

She tip-toed into the master bedroom to check up on the sleeping angel. Swirling trails of black slime glistened all over the pillows and sheets. So my baby drools, she thought. So what? All babies drool and poop in their diapers and cry at all hours so nevermind those things. It couldn't get any worse than that, could it? She left the room and walked downstairs to her and Bill's office, mentally calculating the cost of each baby item. She sat at the desk and moved the mouse around, pulling the computer out of sleep mode. A fantasy football window popped up and Joy clicked out of it. Bill had so many fetishes and obsessions. Couldn't she be allowed just this one? She opened a Google window and searched *raising a baby* and scrolled down until she clicked on what promised to be the most reliable guide for new mothers. As the page loaded, she opened two more Google windows, one to check her eBay account and the other to search for nursery ideas. Of course, she already had the entire nursery planned in her head.

Logging onto eBay, it pleased her to discover that a scale replica of the Twin Towers had topped seven hundred dollars. A painting of the same towers, signed by three firefighters, sold for triple that. A few years ago, nobody would have dared forecast such a healthy market for 9/11 memorabilia, but it made Joy a wealthy, independent woman. If demand increased any more, her income would surpass Bill's at CashNet. Ha! To see the look on his face, she thought. Oh, that bastard. He's intolerable sometimes, but I do love him. I really do. The problem lies—

Upstairs, the angel screamed.

TWO

Joy gasped. What had been done to the pillows on the guest bed? Cloth and goose feathers fluttered to the carpet in thin shreds. The pillows her deceased grandmother had sewn now laid in tatters, irreparable. Her heart skipped a beat when she discovered, in the midst of the textile chaos, her crying baby. "There there, sweet angel," she said. "Mommy will make everything better."

Joy scooped the black angel into her arms and rocked it back and forth. Unable to locate ears on the creature, she cooed into its face as she glanced around the room. Panda had probably destroyed the pillows. That damn cat was always getting into trouble. Joy resolved to lock the cat in the den. With a baby around, a housecat could be trusted about as much as a ravenous lion.

The angel screamed in Joy's arms as she left the guest room. She let go of it long enough to close the door. She walked into the master bedroom and nudged the door shut behind her. When she nestled her baby between the sheets, it stopped crying. Joy tried to wipe the tears from its face but the slick film that coated the angel smeared all over her hands.

She entered the master bathroom, but when she found a

dry towel, the black drool had already seeped through her pores. She felt sick again. Even as the room tilted around her, every bone in her body ached to lie beside her angel. She wondered if its slime was unsanitary and instantly scolded herself for thinking such a dreadful thing. She'd have to keep the baby off the counters and kitchen table, but those were no places for a baby anyway.

The telephone rang.

It rang again and she ran to answer it. She grabbed the portable receiver and checked the caller ID. Bill was calling. She let it ring two more times before answering. "What do you want," she said, no longer nauseated but high on angel slime.

There was some shuffling on the other end of the line. A woman moaned. Bill's coital hoots and hollers joined the squealing. Beneath it all, Joy heard the creaks and groans of a bed frame.

She held the phone at arm's distance. Her thumb hovered over the OFF button, but she failed to muster the courage to hang up for good. She racked her brain for something to say. Bill had obviously turned on the speaker, so the other woman would hear anything she said. She wanted to tell him off, but feared the woman might come to the opinion that she was a desperate housewife who listened over the phone as her husband fucked other women.

She listened for another minute before slamming the phone onto the hardwood floor. The phone cracked in two. The only words exchanged had been spoken—rather, shouted—by the anonymous woman. *Fuck me, fuck me.*

Joy kicked the broken phone beneath the bed and collapsed beside the angel. She buried her face in the pillows and sobbed. The angel whined. Joy screamed into the pillow and thought of all the times she had lied to herself about Bill's love for her. After two failed marriages, she was still naïve. She'd made a fool of herself again. She screamed into the pillow and the angel screamed with her. She fumbled along the sheets until she touched the angel's belly. It spit up bile that dribbled down her arm and soaked into the oily shadow the angel had left on the sheets.

She withdrew her arm and tucked it beneath her chin. Warm pinpricks tingled all along her flesh. So much had gone so wrong. At least her angel was here. As the phone rang throughout the house, she chewed the meat between her thumb and index finger until her own blood mixed with the bile. She lapped at the fluids until she blacked out.

Bill called again a few hours later. Joy awoke to the phone still ringing. They talked this time. He was coming home. He would forgive her for the angel if she forgave him for the phone call. Joy failed to understand why she gave in to his offer, but she did and that was that. She preferred not to think about it. She had a baby to care for.

THREE

As Bill fucked her, Joy imagined the woman he'd been with earlier. Her eyes half shut, she saw a redhead of medium height. It must have been Susan, the secretary at CashNet, or a woman just like her. At last year's corporate holiday party, Bill got drunk and openly hit on Susan. Joy had physically unlatched Bill from the secretary and driven home as he sulked in the passenger seat. She'd brushed that night away as the result of a bad reaction between alcohol and Bill's anxiety meds. They never spoke about the incident, but now it dawned on Joy that what she witnessed that night held more import than she originally attributed to it.

Bill and Susan must have taken a motel room or borrowed the loft of a recent grad eager to please the company vets in order to move up the corporate ladder.

Joy hardly felt it when Bill came. She didn't care. She had only consented to his sexual pass because after fucking, Bill grew pacified and childlike. After make-up sex, he always apologized for his mistakes. Sometimes he even sobbed into her chest. He was a sorry bastard and this was how Joy drove that fact into his heart.

Bill offered no apology this time. "Again," he said, squeezing her arms too hard.

The angel cooed in the makeshift pile of bedding Joy had set up in the corner of the room. She felt a pang of guilt for forgetting her baby during sex. A mother should remain constantly aware of her newborn, she thought. There could be no time for personal relations or pleasures.

"I'm too tired," she said. "I need to check on the child."

Bill huffed and rolled off of her. He lit a cigarette and said, "What's its name?"

"Don't smoke around the baby," she said.

"What's its name?"

Joy twisted around to face away from Bill. Had she been so oblivious and self-absorbed that she forgot to name the angel?

The angel cooed and gurgled.

Joy leapt out of bed and ran to it. She scooped it in her arms and rocked it back and forth. "There there," she said. "Mommy's here now. We'll find a name for you."

"Call it Satan," Bill yelled, propped up in bed. "Call it what it is."

The angel screamed in Joy's arms. It vomited onto her bare chest. The bile streamed down her breasts, across her belly, and slid down her legs. It oozed into her skin and ran between her toes, dripping on the hardwood floor. Joy's shoulders tightened as the baby shrieked so loud the windowpanes shook.

The angel trembled and went limp in her arms. It croaked like a toad. It drooled. It clutched Joy's wrist between its tiny hands and whimpered like a dying dog. Joy stepped into the bathroom as Bill shouted *Satan, Satan.*

The moon shone through the bathroom windows and cast half the angel in pale light. The angel puked again. It howled and shrank into the cradle formed by Joy's arms. Bill shouted *Satan, Satan.*

Joy sat on the edge of the bathtub. Bill made her feel like dying. She wanted to kill herself for being such a terrible mother. She lowered her face to the angel's and thought of all the names she'd seen while browsing baby name books in the mall. Dean, James, Scooter . . . they were all so inadequate.

The baby's head fell off, interrupting her ruminations. It fell on the floor and cracked in two. An apple-shaped sponge that must have been the angel's brain quivered between the halves of its skull. Joy lost her balance and fell backwards into the tub, still clutching the oily body to her chest.

A fountain of black ooze spewed from its neck stump, quickly filling the bathtub until the slosh flowed over the edge and crept across the bathroom floor. Joy sank up to her neck in slime. She released the angel's body to resist the force pulling her down.

Bill turned on the bathroom light and cried, "Holy shit!" But it was too late. His legs slipped out from under him and he landed on his back. He flopped and wallowed in the shit, screaming *Satan, Satan.*

Joy finally pulled herself out of the bathtub and slid across the floor. She scooped up the baby's brain and shuffled out of the bedroom as Bill continued to shout on the floor.

She took the stairs two at a time until she got to the entryway. As she did whenever Bill got mad and they argued, she went into their office to the left of the entry. She locked the door behind her and held the angel's brain in her lap. She'd had no time to throw on clothes, but her bathrobe hung on the back of the swivel chair. She set the brain on the desk and put on the robe. It wasn't much help. Coated from her neck to her toes in tar-like sludge, the robe clung to every inch of her. As the slime soaked into her skin, the robe hung on like epidermal flesh.

She moved two small bookcases in front of the door for reinforcement. When she turned around, the brain had already doubled in size. Boils swelled up all over the brain, then tiny arms and legs sprouted to form a lion's mane of limbs. Eyes— emerald green eyes—blinked open on the tip of each arm and leg. In the center of the limbs, right on the brain's belly, yawned a mouth of chiseled yellow teeth.

Joy realized her baby was not dead, just growing.

And she thought of a name. She wasn't sure where it came from. Maybe from all of the black filth she had taken in. Certainly not from one of those books. It had come to her as if from a cathode ray sent by the angel itself. She smiled and started to cry. She scooped the tentacled brain into her arms and said, "I will name you Abel."

FOUR

Joy huddled beneath the desk as Bill pounded on the office door. He threatened to kill the angel and burn down the house. The angel sat on one of the bookshelves propped against the door. As its limbs smacked and rubbed against the door, its eyes remained fixed on Joy.

Abel's metamorphosis continued. He grew lobster claws and wings coated in obsidian fish scales. A long, needle-spiked tongue hung out of his mouth. Joy didn't want to interfere with her baby's natural growth cycle. Otherwise, she would have held him in her arms. At least Bill's ruckus didn't frighten him.

The door wavered in its frame. It wouldn't hold out much longer. It seemed paper-thin. Joy sobbed into her hands as she considered what Bill would do when he busted down the door. He might kill or torture the innocent child.

"Open the door, honey," Bill yelled. "I have a right. I'm your husband."

"Go take your pills, Bill," Joy said.

"It's too late for that," he said, ceasing his pounding. He must have exhausted himself. "Open the door."

"No," she said. "Not until you calm down."

"I am calm," he shouted.

"You're furious," she said. "You can't be calm if you're furious."

"Give me a break," he said, and stomped away.

Abel burped. He pulled a book from the shelf and groped several pages before tossing it to the floor. The book landed a few feet from Joy. It was The Idiot's Guide to the Bible.

Joy heard Bill on the staircase. She crawled out from beneath the desk and inched toward the office door. She grabbed one of Abel's hands and pressed her lips to his forehead. As she kissed him, Abel cooed and hopped off the bookshelf. He pawed at Joy to move the bookshelves. She shook her head left and right. "I'm sorry, baby," she said. "Daddy is a bad man. We can't trust him."

The angel whimpered and pushed on the bookshelf. It did not budge. The angel whipped its tongue against the spine of a book. The needle tongue pierced the teal hardback jacket and flipped the book into the air. It sailed through the air and banged—muffled, rather—against the far wall. Richard Ellis's Monsters of the Sea, Joy noted. It had been a gift from Papa Haniver shortly before his death. The book had never been read. She only kept it for sentimental purposes.

Abel lowered his head and charged the door. He rammed into the shelves blocking it, then collapsed on the floor and cried. Joy scooped her baby in her arms. She scolded herself once more for being a negligent mother. She inspected Abel's head but found no sign of a serious wound. The angel pointed a claw at the door and sobbed what sounded to Joy like a close approximation of *mama*.

"Mama's right here, mama will take care of you," she said.

The angel screamed. The window rattled and cracked vertically.

Joy shuddered. She debated lowering the blinds to hide the cracked window from Bill until she could get it replaced, but Abel twisted her hair between his claws and yanked hard. She yelped and nearly dropped the baby. "Alright, sweetheart," she said. "Are you sleepy? Are you hungry? Oh, you must be. I'm sorry you have such a careless mother."

She set Abel on the floor and slid the shelves away from the door. Abel clapped his hands together and leaped up, hurrying to open it. He didn't even wait for Joy as he scuttled out of the office and into the entryway. Breathless and fearful of what Bill might do to the child, Joy followed as the angel struggled up the stairs one step at a time.

Abel nudged the door and slithered into the master bedroom. Joy leaned against the doorframe and wiped her sweaty palms on her damp robe. Bill lay on the bed, jerking off and holding a phone to his ear. It was getting light now.

"Show some decency," Joy said. She scooped Abel off the floor and cradled him.

Bill muttered into the receiver and hung up. He flung the phone into the bathroom. It skidded across the tile and cracked three ways against the bottom of the counter. Joy bit her bottom lip and sat on the edge of the bed. She faced away from Bill but tilted her head at such an angle that he remained in her periphery. His penis started to go limp and he pulled the burgundy comforter waist-high.

He said, "Come to bed."

"I'm not tired," she said.

"You're not tired because you're crazy. Crazy people never sleep."

Joy rocked Abel in her arms. The angel stared back at her, alert but silent. "You never slept before they put you on medication. Were you crazy?"

"Get over the insect and come to bed. I won't stand for it."

"Why should I trust you? I stopped loving you."

"You can't stop loving me."

Joy sighed and curled up with Abel on the bed. She craned her neck. Bill was staring at her. "When did you stop loving me?" he said.

She tilted her head to her left shoulder. "I don't know. Last year, maybe."

"Since last year," Bill said.

"Maybe the year before last, or yesterday. It's all the same if I don't love you."

"If you don't love me," Bill said.

Now Joy cried. She cried because if she no longer loved Bill, then the last six years had been wasted nurturing this disaster. She had fallen head over heels for Bill, and he for her. All of that fled long ago, she realized. It was so easy to mistake love's ruins for the real thing, but even as she thought this, her terror of isolation engulfed her. She barfed on the angel.

"For Christ's sake," Bill said, hopping out of bed. "You're pitiful. You're pitiful, you know that? Just pitiful."

He dressed in the bathroom in the dark. Joy rolled her head in vomit and sobbed. She puked herself into a black smear of stars. Abel slipped from her grasp and the stars smothered her.

FIVE

Laughter in the daylight.

Joy scratched at the bile that caked her eyes shut. Her chest ached. Laughter again. It hurt to breathe. The laughter came from the stairs. She opened her eyes. She got out of bed and slipped out of her robe, into a white paisley dress on the floor. She staggered from the bed to the door, the door to the stairs. Her eyes took another minute to adjust to the sunlight washing everything in a golden pale haze.

First she saw Abel sitting on the top step, and she remembered the previous night. But she hardly recognized Abel. He had undergone another transformation. Not only was he laughing, her baby was now three feet tall. The tentacles with their emerald eyes still waved all over his body and his scales glinted darkly, but his wings had fallen off. The skeleton of an umbrella had sprouted where his head used to be. It twirled, perhaps to the rhythm of the angel's thoughts, or for no reason at all.

A booger hand unfurled from Abel's chest and pointed a webbed finger at the banister. Joy laughed. It was so wonderful to hear her baby boy laugh. She had been concerned about abnormal development and laughter was a good indication of a normal, healthy child. She laughed louder because Abel pointed to a very funny thing. A cat's tail wrapped around the banister and stretched over the edge, beyond her line of sight. She stepped forward to get a look at this curious and *oh, how funny* thing. It hurt to breathe but Joy screamed anyway because Bill looked so absurd on *that* side of the railing. She laughed and screamed and nearly fell down the stairs. The cat disappeared into the back of Bill's skull and jutted out of his mouth. Panda's head poked right through Bill's split-wide jaws. His eyeballs dangled from the cat's front paws, which had penetrated his sockets from behind. They had crusted over, much like Joy's eyes. The top of Bill's skull bulged, probably because his brain now had to accommodate the cat's bulk in that cramped space. Bill wore a Raiders jersey and no pants.

So what if Abel killed Bill? Abel was her son and Bill had proven himself untrustworthy and unloving. She could not fear her son. She could not afford to. She used to fantasize nightmare scenarios where Bill died or left her, abandoning Joy to the sideshow horrors that tormented lonely people. She had feared Bill's loss more than any of the heinous acts he committed because Joy thoroughly hated herself. Now that her husband was dead, the situation necessitated that she shift every atom in her body to motherhood. Otherwise, Abel might leave. Not that he had anywhere to go, for he was only a child, but he might run away or call child services. Abel's actions betrayed no sign that he might turn on her, and she swore to appease him at all costs. That meant taking care of business, beginning with the most important thing in constructing a young person's moral foundation: education.

Bill's corpse could hang there for a while. The cat's tail held pretty strong. Also, Ronald Reagan Elementary School was only a few blocks away. Abel could be on the fast track to knowledge in no time.

"I am glad," she said, trembling and very frightened. "I am blessed with a beautiful son."

He would need to be properly dressed for his big first day, so Joy found her car keys and purse. She compared the country club virtue of the polo shirt to the lumberjack charm of flannel. She ushered Abel downstairs and out the front door.

SIX

They waited outside of Macy's at the Valley Plaza until a short, wiry man with a shaved head opened the door. His nametag said he was Kevin Donihe, store manager. Joy nudged Abel from behind, urging him to walk by the man, but Kevin blocked their path. He rubbed his tired, baggy eyes and stared at Abel. "Are you treating a trickster," he said, "or tricking a treatster?"

"We're looking for the children's section," Joy said.

The manager looked nervous. He sidestepped toward a rack of ties, dropped to his knees, and disappeared. From the tie rack, he called out, "Second floor, but be on guard! My guru says a happy demon lives up there."

Joy thanked the manager and hurried toward the escalator. What a crazy little man, she thought.

The second floor was devoted entirely to children's clothes, half for boys and half for girls. She took a few steps toward the boy's section. When she looked behind her, she realized that he had gone ahead. He headed directly for a line of dresses. She went after him.

"Those aren't for you," she said, grabbing a tentacle. He slapped her hand away and yanked a striped green and yellow dress off a hanger.

She watched as his goop sank into the flesh of her palm. She shut her eyes and rubbed her temples. When she opened her eyes, she glanced around and noticed that no other customers milled about. Nobody stood behind the cash register. This spared her some embarrassment. She had never taught Abel that boys and girls wear different clothes, that breaking the clothing conduct can result in mockery, insults, and social exile. Maybe he can wear a dress just this once, she thought. If I don't buy it for him, he will be upset. He might hate me. It would be unfair to deny him what he wants without first teaching him why he cannot have it.

"Alright, get the dress," she said. "Make sure it fits."

Abel had already slipped it over his head. He pressed his tentacles against the fabric, cutting holes for his many limbs. His slime seeped through the dress, darkening the green and yellow to shades of brown.

"Can I help you with anything?" said a voice behind them.

Joy spun around. It was Kevin. He wore a grinning Chinese demon mask. She stood in front of Abel to block him from the manager's view. "What are you doing?" she said.

"I am the happy demon. I am here to assist all customers. With my wisdom and guidance, you will find the ultimate purchase."

"Fine then. We need a pair of shoes."

"Baby shoes are on sale for two dollars," the manager said.

"My son is not a baby."

"Rattlesnake boots are fifty percent off."

"Are they fashionable?"

"The forefront of fashion. More popular than roller-skate shoes."

"A pair of those sounds swell. You can leave us alone now. We've had all the help we need."

The store manager in the demon mask clapped his hands and moonwalked toward the escalator, backwards. A moment after he vanished from sight, he cried out. Joy cringed as she listened to his yelps. He had tripped and fallen on the escalator. She considered helping him, but decided to find the rattlesnake boots first. Another employee should be around to help him.

They came to the boot display in no time. Abel seemed overjoyed by them. At least he wasn't a hopeless cause. Joy sat him down on a bench and slid a boot onto each of his feet. "How precious," she said. She hoped wearing such stylish boots would balance out how silly he looked in a dress. Then maybe other children wouldn't make fun of him. "Let's ring up and get you to school."

They stepped on the escalator. Joy bit her lip as she realized that the step they stood on was actually the store manager. Somehow, after his fall, he must have gotten sucked into the machine and turned into a cubic step of man and demon mask.

They walked out of the store without paying for Abel's outfit and nobody was around to stop them.

Joy turned the car into the pick-up loop in front of the school office. A few latecomers hurried through the halls and parking lot. "Hurry now, honey," she said. "You want to be on time for your first day."

She kissed the skeleton of Abel's umbrella and felt a twinge of regret. She would have to be away from her baby for an entire afternoon.

Joy drove away after Abel turned down a corridor and

vanished in the grid of stucco classrooms. She hoped the school accepted unregistered students. It was the beginning of October. School had not been in session for very long. Surely no kindergarten teacher would deny the virtues of education to any child, especially a boy as loving and well-behaved as Abel.

Back home, Joy made a pot of coffee, scrambled two eggs, and toasted a slice of rye. She piled the eggs on the bread and sat at the kitchen table. She took a bite and found the bread tasteless and stale. She sprinkled pepper and salt onto the eggs and toast and ate her meal in quiet thought. The bread still tasted stale.

Joy put her left elbow on the table and pinched the bridge of her nose. She hardly believed her husband had died on such a breezy October day. She knew people died all the time, every day in fact, but it seemed unnatural that anyone could die on a perfect autumn day. Those days rarely came and never lasted. It was plain misfortune to die on one. Maybe I'm wrong, Joy thought. Maybe those are the days given to us for the sole purpose of dying. Anyway, she needed to catch up on her eBay auctions and would have no time to fetch Bill and Panda from the stairs until evening.

SEVEN

The morning and early afternoon slipped by until the phone rang. Joy glanced at the clock as she reached for the phone. "Already three?" she said, recoiling from the phone. "How did I let this happen?"

She scooped up her keys and rushed out of the house, but the phone never stopped ringing. She hesitated in the driveway. What if it was an important call? She ran back into the house. The phone still rang. She took it off the receiver and slowly lifted it to her ear. "Hello?" she said.

Hoarse breathing on the other end.

"Who is this?"

"Bill Erickson is dead." It was two voices speaking in unison.

"How do you know that? Tell me your names."

"Give us the angel."

"There's no angel here. Why are you calling?"

"When an angel kills, we are the first to know."

"How did you get this number?"

"We are willing to negotiate a deal. If you do not return the angel, rest assured, Bill will return."

"You fucking creeps. I'm calling the police."

Joy hung up the phone.

She screeched to a halt in front of the school office. Abel sat on the sidewalk, slumped over and spinning his umbrella head with his hands. He stood, walked to the car, and opened the door. Despite the parking lot full of cars, Joy saw no parents or teachers. She saw no children but Abel. He climbed into the car and they sped away.

"How was your day, darling?" Joy said.

Abel hissed. Joy guessed that meant the other kids took as kindly to him as they typically did with students who began after the start of the school year. She recalled her own move from her father's apartment in Chicago to live with her mother in Lone Pine, California. The children of that lonesome, unattractive town didn't even speak to Joy until her fourth month at Eagle Elementary. It had taken that long for them to determine that she wasn't the weird little alien girl they initially took her for. "I suppose some things never change," Joy said. She patted a tentacle and said, "Be happy, Abel. Mommy knows kids can be mean, but let them act dumb and immature. You just keep on being the shining, precious thing you are. They'll realize their mistake soon enough. Then those little idiots will be knocking on our door every day, begging to play with you."

"I ate the school," Abel said. They were his first real words.

"What was that?" Joy asked, puzzled.

"I ate the school," he said.

"Do you mean you hate school? I bet those snot brains said some bad things to you on the playground, but hate is a strong word. I don't care if you heard it from someone or whatever awful things they said. I will not tolerate my own child romping around as a hatemonger. If you have a problem with someone, you should talk to me or say something to your teacher. What's your teacher's name? Did you find your classroom alright?"

"I ate the school," Abel insisted.

"Oh, I get it. You ate in the school cafeteria. Silly mommy. She's so oblivious sometimes." She pulled into the driveway. A black Town Car was parked in front of the house. She failed to notice it when she drove to the school. Must've been in a hurry. Nonetheless, it put a sour sickness in her stomach.

Inside the house, Joy put a bowl of instant macaroni and cheese in the microwave. She started a load of laundry so that Abel's dress would be clean for the next day. She turned on the television and found a stop-motion cartoon about camels sitting in an empty white room. Abel sat a foot away from the television. His tentacles slapped against the screen. Although Joy disapproved of children sitting so close to televisions—blindness and cancer were true risks, after all—it gladdened her that he enjoyed the program.

The microwave beeped. She removed the bowl from the microwave and a spoon from the silverware drawer. She set the macaroni and cheese on the floor beside Abel. As he splattered black slime across the two-dimensional images of silent, unfeeling camels, it occurred to Joy that this was the first real meal she had ever prepared for her son. I must be the worst mother on earth, she thought.

Abel reached a hand into the bowl and showered his umbrella head with the orange, artificially flavored noodles.

A sticky white fluid squirted from the umbrella ends and the noodles disintegrated into the child's wiry head. What an individual eater, Joy thought. What fortune to be blessed with such a unique son.

They spent the rest of the day sitting on the floor, watching the camel people do nothing and mashing noodles and cheese powder into their skulls.

EIGHT

All the next morning, after she dropped Abel off for his second day of school, Joy moped around the house, incapable of fulfilling eBay orders or even folding the laundry she'd started yesterday. In such a short time, her attachment to Abel had swelled to encompass everything. Their bond shrouded every aspect of Joy. On one hand, she loved being a mother. It meant more to her than anything this world could offer. She resisted the nagging sense that she was trapped. Since she could remember, Joy had suffered from a peculiar claustrophobia concerning people. Her readiness to embrace love always went too far. The closer she got to a person, the more strangled she felt until it reached a breaking point, and she fled. With Bill, she managed to overcome her skittishness for the first time, not because of any outstanding qualities she perceived in him, but out of stubbornness and hard work. As with anyone trying to improve themselves, the right self-help books aided Joy's actualization of desired personal growth.

Now the claustrophobia returned in full force.

She realized that if motherhood wasn't enough to murder this feeling once and for all, nothing could save her. I'm selfish, she thought. I'm selfish and unfit to be a mother. Joy fought to repress these judgments as she tuned out to the stop-motion camel cartoon, which she made sure to Tivo this time. She left the house at a quarter 'til noon, two hours before she expected

Abel to leave class.

She parked in front of the school, taking a space in the row closest to the main office. Although she knew school policies required all visitors to check in, she didn't see how taking a quick gander around would hurt anyone.

The brick halls appeared drab and worn in the pale October sun. They offered no sign that children in classrooms racked their brains to hold in all the wisdom of textbooks, no sign of laughter or life. Joy turned a corner, giddy about the possibility of being caught without a visitor's pass.

What she saw made her knees weak. She had to scream to keep from falling down. Child-sized cocoons lined both sides of the hallway, leading straight to the cafeteria. She forced herself to approach them, to figure out what was really going on. Closer up, she saw that each cocoon contained an adult or child. They were dormant beneath the clear, dark layer of phlegm. She reached out to touch a cocoon encasing a little girl and found the texture identical to Abel's slime. Her skin absorbed it and everything became clear to hear. This was an art project. Bearing the mark of Abel, it was obviously his art project.

A torrent of happiness and terror swelled in her chest, quickening her heartbeat to an intolerable speed. She fled the hallway, hurried to the car, and wept against the steering wheel.

A few minutes before three, the insect angel marched out of the desolate school. Joy did not mention the art project. Abel may have intended it to be a surprise. She hoped he would invite her to see it whenever it was complete. And she no longer felt smothered, which meant Abel could not be the object smothering her. As long as he sat beside her, she basked in motherly love.

As soon as she turned onto their street, the black car that had posted up in front of the house the previous day appeared behind them. "How about some ice cream?" Joy said.

She jerked the steering wheel hard to the left, nearly clipping the mailman as he marched across the street. Joy apologized to his blue-suited figure in the side view mirror. Envelopes and packages scattered around him. A sheaf of junk mail floated away on the gutter's current.

And the black car followed.

They finally found a place to park in the cramped lot of the ice cream shop, but the black car had beaten them there. Joy did not know how this was possible. The plan to take Abel out for ice cream had been spontaneous. Unless they had implanted a tracking device inside the car or—God forbid—on Abel, how could they know? Joy looked over at Abel. His head spun silently.

She toyed with other, less sinister reasons that might result in the followers ending up at the same ice cream joint. True, it was nearby. October was actually a popular ice cream month, when people reminisced about the loss of another summer, finally laying it to rest in a cold, pre-winter scoop of their favorite childhood flavor. Yes, everybody ate ice cream in October. Even creeps who stalked single mothers and demanded they give up the most precious thing on earth, their only child.

If she and Abel went into the shop, they would be in a public place, surrounded by happy people. That counted for something. That meant they were safe. She might even catch sight of the followers. Then she could hand their identities over to the police. Everyone in the world would stand behind Joy and Abel, innocent mother and son. If they walked into the ice cream shop, all their troubles of the last twenty-four hours might end forever. The dead husband troubles would remain, but nobody believed the testaments of stalking creeps. Joy could blame the death on them. They were criminals, after all.

She got out of the car and walked around to the passenger side. She opened the door for Abel, leaned over to unbuckle his seatbelt, and one day passed into the next.

NINE

"You better not have any homework due today," Joy said, turning into the pickup loop in front of the school office. "A good impression is key to lasting success. Oh, nevermind. It's my fault for letting you watch all that television. Have a good day, sweetie. I'll see you after class." She kissed Abel's umbrella and he hopped out of the car.

It was eight in the morning and silent. Cars filled the parking lot. Everywhere she looked, an emptiness confronted her. She sighed. Despite the warm autumn air, the chills crept over her. Joy squeezed the steering wheel and overcame the impulse to start smoking again. She resisted and turned the radio louder. She could not allow six years to go down the drain that fast. A radio host said something funny and laughed. Joy missed the remark but laughed anyway. Another person laughed and made a witticism that she failed to understand. She found humor in none of it. None of it made sense. Anyway, she laughed. That was common and universal enough that despite all the nightmare dread of facing an empty house, where loneliness and self-loathing lurked behind every door, she could partake in the laughter. Otherwise, the anxiety of waiting for three o'clock to arrive was pure misery.

She stopped laughing when she pulled into the driveway.

TEN

Two dark-suited figures burst out of the house as Joy sat in her car in the driveway. They ran across the front lawn, jumped into the Lincoln Town Car parked in front of the house, and sped off. Joy wasn't so sure, but the men looked awfully like

Camel Joe, or the stop-motion camels from the cartoon. She brushed this off as a displacement of her cigarette craving and killed the engine. She got out of the car.

The front door hung wide open. Everything seemed to be in proper order, so Joy searched harder. Nobody broke into a house and left things untouched. She knew what dark intentions aroused home invasion. These men wanted money, jewels, and God knew what else. "Thieves," she screamed. "Thieves!" She stormed from the entryway to the office, the kitchen to the living room. She returned to the entryway and dashed up the stairs, yelling all the while. "Thieves! Outlaws! Invaders!"

Joy regretted her reluctance to ever activate the home security system. Bill always insisted— She halted at the top of the staircase. The corpses no longer hung from the banister.

She stumbled into the master bedroom. Gray light poured in from the windows on the far wall, illuminating the dust that floated between the glass panes and the bed propped against the adjacent wall.

Bill's hands and feet were nailed to the mattress. He was the spitting image of a blue collar savior, except for his head. The men who broke in must have taken that with them. They'd severed Bill's head and shoved two cat paws into his neck. The paws jutted out like furry antennas.

In a lightning instant of recognition, Joy ran out of the room and down the stairs as fast as she could. The toe of her left shoe caught on one of the middle steps and she tumbled the rest of the way down. Her head slammed against the entryway floor. She got up and ran out the door, pulling the keys from her pocket. The front door stood ajar behind her, but that no longer mattered. She knew in her heart that the men in dark suits already scoured every classroom of the school, searching for Abel.

ELEVEN

Without understanding how or why, Joy found herself outside the cafeteria's double doors. She failed to remember the drive here. Abel had expressed so much enthusiasm for eating at school. Maybe that explained why she came to the cafeteria, which stood on the far edge of the school, away from the office, classrooms, and twisted hallways. Perhaps it had something to do with his special, secret cocoon project and how the bodies led right up to the cafeteria.

She pushed through the doors and entered the building. The air in the room hung thick and sticky. She held a hand over her mouth until she learned to take shallower breaths so the air would not stick in her lungs.

In the center of the cafeteria, between the long bench rows, two human-headed earwigs writhed on the floor.

Children sat on the benches, unmoving and rigid. Black slime smothered their faces and clothes.

The earwigs howled. They paid no attention to Joy as they fucked. Their legs fell off and turned to dust. Their ribs liquefied into swamp-colored tar that reeked of gasoline. Joy turned her gaze to the stage at the far end of the cafeteria. Abel stood center stage. He raised his tentacles to the ceiling, umbrella spinning, and chanted nonsense.

Joy ran across the room, maneuvering around the earwigs. She pulled herself onto the stage and took her son in her arms. He pushed her away and ceased talking gibberish long enough to say, "No, mommy."

Joy stiffened. He called me mommy, she thought. This little miracle crippled her. So much happiness swelled through her that even as her son approached the human-headed earwigs tonguing in the midst of coitus, she believed everything must be okay. Abel is an intelligent child, she thought. He will do what is good and safe.

The insect angel stopped a foot away from the earwigs. He

fell to his knees. His tentacles quivered and snorted tar and leg dust through their many eyes. When the powder and liquid diminished, Abel sprawled on his back and convulsed.

"Abel!" Joy said. She jumped offstage.

The earwigs spurted something like putty out of their mouths. As if appalled by the horror of copulation, they rolled off of each other and died.

Joy's footsteps echoed in the cafeteria. She fell on the floor and gathered Abel's tentacled body to her chest. "Abel," she said.

The cafeteria doors creaked open. The dark-suited men stood in the doorway. As they stepped into the room, Joy squinted through the haze and saw that she had not been wrong. They were camel people, identical to the ones in the stop-motion cartoon. She said to herself that such things did not exist beyond nightmares, but they stood there all the same. The fact was that camel people did exist, and they wanted her child.

The camel men paced across the room in jerky spasms, moving like puppets. Both of them held a glowing book in their hands. Joy shook Abel to wake him. He remained unconscious.

Ten feet away, the camel people stopped, opened their mouths, and spit globs of silky phlegm. Their spit overshot Joy and Abel. It splattered across the face of a dead earwig.

The earwig's skull cracked in two, emitting a flurry of bats made of cheese. The camel people did not spit a second time. They seemed as mesmerized as Joy by the bats.

The bats scattered. Each of them homed in on a particular child and squeezed between the lips of that child, disappearing into their adolescent mouths. Instantly, young unfeeling eyes flickered alert at every table. Without bothering to wipe the slime from their faces, the children linked arms in a circle around Abel and Joy.

The camel men exchanged a glance and grunted. They

spoke in unison. "Miss Erickson, the angel is a betrayer of God. Hand him over and let Heaven have the final word."

Joy pulled Abel closer. She could only see the faces of the camel men because the children blocked her view of the rest of them. "Get out of here, you freaks," she said. "I will not give you my son. You are not messengers from God. You are murderers, thieves, home invaders."

"Give us the child," they said.

"Demons, get out!"

"The angel will betray you," they said.

"You liars," Joy said, "you crazy animals." She wept and shrieked. She could take no more lunacy from these camel people.

"We will be seeing you," they said, and walked out of the cafeteria.

The children held hands and fixed their eyes on Joy until Abel's umbrella started twirling again. They broke their circle to allow the mother and insect angel to pass out of it. Horrifying as she found them, Joy felt indebted to these children. Without their protection, who could say what the camel people might have done?

The children walked in single-file rows to the left and right of Joy and Abel. The two in the lead pushed open the cafeteria doors and ushered the other children to form their circle again. In this way, they entered the labyrinthine halls of the school.

It was dark now. Children and adults lay cocooned all down the hallway. All of these dead or comatose people were headless. They had not been headless before Joy held a hand over her mouth, understanding what Abel meant when he said he ate the school. This had been no special art project. Certainly child protective services would want a word with her. What kind of home life stirred such monstrous urges?

They turned left at a forked hall and the main office came into view, just fifty yards ahead.

The office door opened. The camel people tiptoed into the hallway, blocking the path. One of them held Bill's head in its paws. "Give us the child," the camels said.

The camel holding the head crouched into bowling stance and swung its arm back and forth, then released the head. Bill's head—a mutilated grin frozen on his face—rolled toward the circle of children. It bowled over a child in the front, breaking his legs before passing between Joy and Abel, narrowly missing them. The head slammed into a child in the back, crushed her legs, and tumbled down a hallway.

Except for the two children with broken legs, all of the others giggled. Without any warning, they cried out, "Crawl inside the devils!"

The children chased after the camel people, who turned and puppet-hopped past the front office. Joy took Abel by a tentacle. They followed after the children. Whatever their purpose, the children frightened the camels.

When the camel people disappeared over a brick wall, the children returned and huddled around her. They followed Joy to her car and piled into the back seat one after another like clowns.

They drove home.

TWELVE

The front door was shut now. Someone had been there. Someone had closed the door. The children in front of the circle pushed it open. Despite her protests, the children behind Joy pushed her and Abel into the house. They locked the door and dispersed, turning on lights in every room. Some of them ran upstairs. Other children ran into rooms on the first floor. Everywhere, Joy heard doors creak open and bang shut.

Abel scuttled out of the entryway, toward the living room. Joy reached for him. He slipped out of her grasp. She followed, halting in her tracks when she saw the camel men. They stood side by side outside the back door. They smashed their noses against the glass and breathed heavy enough to obscure their faces in clouds of moisture. She backed against the pantry door.

Abel turned the television on. He switched to the show about the camels in the white room and plopped down on the floor. The camels opened their golden Bibles and opened their jaws. Although they spoke in unison, they read from different sections. The discord between their words and their voices entranced the insect angel. Joy feared he was being brainwashed, but her faith in Abel gave her the strength to believe that no television show could ever brainwash him, no matter what tactics were used by the media conglomerates behind the show.

A hideous elephant-like bellow came from upstairs, followed by the scuffle of sneakers

The children came into the living room, dragging a camel man by his legs. They pinned the camel man to the floor. It looked about wild-eyed as the real-life camels watched from the back door. Abel remained fixated on the cartoon.

One child, a little boy, stroked the camel man's head. The boy plugged the camel's nostrils with his thumbs and lowered his face to the creature's mouth. His head vanished between the camel's jaws, snuffing its yelps.

The boy slipped all the way into the camel person. The children released the body and turned their attention to the television. The boy in the camel rose to his feet. Joy cried out and ducked into the pantry. She craned her head around the door and stared on as a tentacle broke out of the creature boy's skull. Its head fell off and rolled across the floor. It was a puppet's head, made out of coarse fabric and wire. Two tentacles burst from the shoulders and the camel's arms sailed across the room in opposite directions. The camel's body doubled over and then rose again. It exploded. Stuffing, spit, and wire shot across the living room and kitchen.

When the stuffing settled, Joy saw what had been made of the boy. Tentacles identical to Abel's swung from his body, which had melted into a flesh column of eyeless children's faces. A tentacle hung from each of the child-mouths. Black slime oozed from the top of the column, where a bald, pale head spun on a green plastic spinal chord that jutted into the body. With each rotation, the head smiled at Joy, grinning a mouthful of long white teeth that squirmed like slugs.

Joy shut the pantry door and puked in the dark.

A knock on the pantry door startled her awake. She had fallen into restless half-sleep and dreamed about a mannequin skinning her in a carnival funhouse. The knocker rapped against the door again. She pulled herself up by the shelves and turned the handle.

Black slime covered the sofas and floor. It rolled down the walls and dripped from the ceiling.

Abel bent over and greeted her with an umbrella kiss on top of her head. He now stood over ten feet tall. His tentacles stretched long and slender, spanning half the distance of the open kitchen and living room. The pale-faced child monolith stood beside him. Its rubbery teeth fluttered with each rasp it exhaled.

Children sat at the kitchen table. Others sat on barstools at the counter. Most of them sat in front of the television, watching the camel people in the white room. The camels on the television turned their heads, pointed at Joy, and laughed. Their Bibles fell off the screen, into the static white of TV Land.

Take control of the situation, Joy thought. They will pull me under if I do not take control of the situation. Take control. Breathe and take control. Take deep breaths.

Take control.

Take control.

113

Take control.
Take control.
Take control.
Take control.
Take control.
Control.
Control.
Control.

Joy sprung alert. She clapped her hands and smiled at Abel. "How would you and your friends like to play a game?" If she could distract them for long enough, she could probably find a way to get rid of the camel people and contact the parents of the child monolith.

THIRTEEN

"It is time to go," Abel said, pointing at the television. "It is time to go to Heaven."

The camel people were still laughing. Joy understood none of it. She tried to recall a time when her life did not consist of camel people and crazy children. She wanted life to be just her and Abel again. He'd grown up so fast and now she had another child to raise and protect from dangerous people. The world was full of danger. "What do you mean we'll go to Heaven?" Joy said.

"I was born there," Abel said.

"Sweetheart, you can't go to Heaven," Joy said.

"My brother returned and we have our followers now. We must return and conquer. *Those ones* in the television," he slapped a tentacle against the screen, "they do not belong there."

"Oh, but that's not Heaven. That's a television show. It's just make-believe."

"No, mommy. It is Heaven."

Joy realized that she should play along with her son. Once he realized that going inside a television show was impossible, she could take him to a toy store and see if they carried any camel people action figures. Seeing how the show was popular among the children, she figured it must be the current hit cartoon. "Alright," she said, "we can go to Heaven."

"We are going, but you cannot go with us," Abel said.

"What do you mean I can't come with you?"

"Only angels go to Heaven."

"Abel, it isn't nice to exclude your mother."

The children turned to each other and mockingly said, "Abel, it isn't nice to exclude your mother."

Abel wrapped his tentacles around the child monolith. "Mother is a bitch. You should marry her."

"Don't you use that language, young man!" Joy said.

"Or strangle her," the child monolith said.

"Yes, strangle her," Abel said.

Joy gasped. The presence of this ghastly *thing* had changed her sweet baby into a monster. She loved Abel so much. She wanted to take him into her arms and flee the house, but there were still the camel people to worry about. Horrors within and horrors without, she thought. My life is one big horror show. "Okay, okay. Get with it," she said, accidentally speaking aloud.

"Mommy is talking to herself again," Abel said.

"What's that supposed to mean, you little snot?" Joy said. Her own words repelled her.

"Come on," he said, pulling the monolith with him. "Leave her with the minions. The holy passage should be ready soon."

Abel floated across the room and smashed the television. The screen flashed bright white. The camel people sitting in the room became real, identical to the ones cramped in televisions outside the back door. Abel spit lava-flows of black slime as he and his brother skipped tentacle in tentacle out of the living room, coating the entire house in drippy darkness.

FOURTEEN

Joy took a few steps toward the hallway, but something in the living room caught her eye. The camel people reached out of the broken television, pressing buttons on the front panel as if to change the channel on themselves. They toyed with every button until finding the right one. Joy froze as one of the camels belted out an opera-howl sheathed in static.

The glass of the back door shattered. The camels outside clapped their puppet hands. Two camels crawled out of the living room television. Joy backpedaled and tripped over a chair. The child sitting in the chair fell onto the floor beside her. The camel people staggered between children.

They stood over Joy and the fallen child. For a reason unknown to Joy, the television camels were immune to the children, although they licked their chops and drooled as they eyed the slimy little bodies.

"God hath mercy on those who weep," the camel people chanted. "God hath mercy on those who obey the will of the law. Give us the angel or be struck by lightning in your mind."

"Torture somebody else," Joy said. "I'll call the cops on you." Of course, she knew she couldn't really call the cops. She was a child abductor now. She was no better than the criminals she feared and hated. Well, of course she was better than them. She had to be. She knew herself deep down and saw a good heart.

The camels spit. Their phlegm sailed through the air in slow motion. Three children lifted Joy to her feet. They stepped in front of her and blocked the camels' spit attack. As the children disintegrated into thousands of earwigs, the fallen child pulled Joy by the hand into the office at the end of the hallway. The child locked the door and motioned for her to help it slide a bookcase in front of the door.

The camel people pounded on the door, but it held better

than it had under the beatings of Bill. Joy looked around the office, cringing at the stacks of unfulfilled eBay orders. How did I get locked in here again, she wondered. Well, now business would surely tank, and with a weirdo mutant leading her son down a dark path, nothing could be done anymore. She may as well give up.

The child scurried around the room, picking up packages meant to be mailed. It pushed the computer aside and stacked the parcels on the desk. On top of the mountain of boxes, the child shoved books taken from the shelves.

Joy crinkled her brow, truly puzzled. The child crawled onto the makeshift tower and Joy reached out to grab her. "Get down from there. It's not safe," she said.

The camel people gave up on the door. Joy hesitated between the door and the girl. Certainly the camels headed for Abel now.

The girl drew her index finger along the ceiling and traced an octagon in black slime. "There are many paths to Heaven," she said.

The part of the ceiling enclosed by the black octagon melted into air particles, opening a route to the second story. The girl curled her index finger, enticing Joy to step toward her.

The girl gripped two sides of the octagon and lifted herself through the ceiling. Her legs dangled for a moment and then disappeared. Joy stood beside the tower and squinted through the ceiling gap. She realized that the little girl was helping her, that she had opened a passage to Abel.

She climbed onto the desk and scaled the boxes and books. It bent and swayed beneath her weight but held steady long enough for her to reach into the octagon and rise out of the office.

She rolled away from the hole and stared up at the ceiling of the guest bedroom. She recalled putting Abel to bed in here, how the cat tore up all the bedding. It occurred to her that maybe the cat was innocent. Abel had been a problem child right from the start. But he's my problem child, Joy thought.

My poor mothering must be the cause of this whole disaster.

She got to her feet. I love him so much that I've done wrong. Where did I go wrong? She looked about for the little girl but saw her nowhere. The door stood slightly ajar, so she assumed the girl already made her way toward Abel and his freak brother.

She left the guest room. Slime oozed down the walls of the hallway. She looked over the staircase and down to the first floor. It was as if everything had been painted black. She tried to forget the irreparable damage that had been done and faced the master bedroom. When she felt ready, after a few deep breaths, she walked inside. Still nailed to the mattress, Bill twitched. Bubbles gurgled up from his wounds and floated into the air. The bubbles began to form letters. They spelled out a message. *I'll be coming for you.*

Joy shuddered. "In Hell you will," she said. She slid against the wall to keep as far from her mutilated husband as possible. She tilted her head to peer into the bathroom. Children sat on the counters and the floor. The shower door hung ajar. Abel's umbrella head whirled over the top of its glass walls. The child monolith bent over at his feet, running its flimsy white teeth into the drain, which melted away, as if the monolith's saliva contained some sort of acid.

The little girl stopped sucking on one of the monolith's tentacles and turned to Joy. "There she is," the girl said, angry. "The intruder came to stop us."

Taken aback, Joy held her hands to her chest. "But that's not true. That isn't true at all. This house belongs to me and my son. Abel, this little girl led me up here and now she's telling me I don't belong. Is she a friend of yours? What kind of joke are you playing?"

Abel pushed his brother aside and stepped out of the shower. He marched up to Joy, wrapped his tentacles around her legs, and swept her off her feet. Joy's skull cracked against the tile. A stabbing pain flowed down her spine. "Mommy, I am sorry to abandon you," Abel said. "I am an angel from Heaven. I only needed you to protect me until I could grow back into my true self. Now I must return. Do not worry. You belong with the television demons. My minions will take you to them. You can be among your own kind again."

"What do you mean?" Joy said. "I am not a camel. I'd give my life for you."

"And you will," Abel said. "The world outside is ready for you to join them again." He returned to the shower. Its floor transformed into a rusted metal tube and he slid down into darkness with his brother and the little girl.

Joy trembled and curled up on the floor. The remaining children took her in their arms, lifted her above their heads, and carried her out of the bathroom. They took her out of the bedroom, down the stairs, across the entryway, and tossed her onto the doorstep. They locked the door and ran back upstairs, leaving Joy alone and forsaken.

FIFTEEN

Joy looked out at the world from the doorstep. Earwigs and sea monsters filled an inky green sky. Longer than school buses, the monsters glinted like oxblood diamonds. She pressed against the front door and pounded on the glass panes. "Abel, open up," she said. "It's your mother. Don't leave your mother out here."

A dark shape moved out of the shadows of the porch. It sat in the rocking chair closest to Joy and rocked slowly. "How did you get off the mattress?" she cried. Her hands slid down the door and rose to her face. "How did you get off the mattress?" She clawed at her eyes until they bled and stung.

Even then, Bill rocked in the chair. The cat paws rising from his neck stub waved at her. The paws clapped together and formed a mouth between their claws. "I promised I'd return," Bill said. "Now let's love each other like we used to do."

Joy clenched her right hand into a fist and punched the glass pane. It shattered, but sliced her hand so badly that she withdrew it before unlocking the door. She pulled a six-inch sliver from the meat between her thumb and index finger. Bill stopped rocking and stood. He ripped out a cat paw and wound up softball-style. Joy turned too late.

The paw latched onto her skull and tore out a clump of hair. She ran down the walkway as the paw scalped her raw and bald. Bill skipped after her, dancing as if he took part in some deranged musical.

She reached the middle of the street and freed herself of the paw. She tossed it behind her and kept running. She ran past the row of mailboxes, past house after house. A block later, she felt too winded to carry on. She turned around. She'd gained a lot on Bill, who hop-staggered far behind her.

She bent over to catch her breath and wiped the blood from her eyes. The monsters in the sky ignored her. They made zero noise as they swirled about up there. It seemed to Joy that they vacuumed up all the normal sounds of a neighborhood.

Joy sucked in a final deep breath and took off jogging with her eyes closed. Blinking hurt too much.

Down the road, she opened her eyes because she could not handle closing them anymore. Running blindly frightened her.

She stopped dead in her tracks.

An army of camel people stuffed into televisions blocked the road.

Behind her, Bill sang in the near distance.

And she realized, as the camels dragged themselves out of the televisions and jaunted toward her, the impossibility of escape.

The camel people pinned her to the asphalt.

Joy prayed that someday she and her child might meet in Heaven, or anywhere beyond this monstrous world. Anywhere at all, without the cruelty, so long as Abel would forgive her.

Deep in her heart, she still felt that somehow she had betrayed him. It could not be the other way around. She refused to believe that this was anyone's fault but her own.

The camel people undressed the woman as the creatures above opened their mouths and sang a lullaby.

THE GREEN MONSTER
AND HIS LONELINESS

The green monster threw a ball for his loneliness to fetch, and when his loneliness ignored the ball, he sat on the cave floor and cried. "You horrible beast," he said. "I'm tired of this. Find another home if you won't play with me."

The loneliness yawned as it uncurled after a noontime siesta in the half shade of the cave's mouth. It licked its fur clean and ignored the green monster.

"Why did I adopt such a terrible loneliness?" said the green monster, moss-colored tears dripping down his face. He stood and walked to the cave mouth. He scooped the loneliness into his arms and kicked its bottom.

The loneliness zoomed over the valley and splashed into the Bored, Bored River. And as soon as it disappeared into that lazy gray water, the green monster realized his mistake, and he called his loneliness back to him.

When the sun fell, the green monster had already phoned every loneliness shelter in town. Luckless, he listened to the dial tone and pretended to hear the voice, that fuzzy silence, of his beloved loneliness.

I am Meat,
I am in Daycare

When Ted Branson called to ask the rate for Susan's daycare service, she never realized his child was a slab of meat. Now the man pushed her aside and lugged his meat-child into her house. "Name's Mr. Branson, but call me Ted," he said. "Should I put him with the other kids, or will you take him from here?"

"Mr. Branson...Ted," Susan said, "I can't take your child. I'm sorry, it's just not..."

She did not want to take the meat, but she could not offend this man. He might have friends with kids, although she doubted he had friends. Who would hang out with a guy who called meat his child? Well, if she was paid to watch kids and this lunatic wanted to pay her to babysit a hunk of cow, she would do it.

"I don't see what the problem could be."

Susan smiled. "Problem? There's no problem here. Bring your son this way and I'll introduce him to the other children."

"Scotty," Ted said.

"Excuse me?"

"My boy's name is Scotty."

"Oh, of course," said Susan. "His name is Scotty."

For the first time, Susan was glad the seven children she

watched were, without exception, idiots.

She led Mr. Branson into the living room. The man dragged the hunk of meat behind him as if it were a reluctant child. Where the hell had the meat come from anyway? Maybe it was just a large rib-eye steak, but Susan had never seen rib-eyes that size before. She watched the seven children watching Alice in Wonderland, their comatose eyes reflecting the purple visage of the Cheshire Cat. "Everyone," she said. "Everyone, I'd like you to meet Scotty."

Haley, a little blonde girl, turned from the television and waved her hands like someone trying to signal a lifeguard. The other kids heard nothing, or pretended to hear nothing.

Children were such little creeps.

Normally, there were over ten pages of paperwork to fill out for a new child, but since Scotty wasn't really a child, she skipped the paperwork.

"Well," Mr. Branson said, "I'm late for work. If there are any forms to sign, I'll fill them out this evening, around five. Thanks again."

He kissed Susan on the cheek. He walked out of the living room. The front door slammed. Susan realized she had forgotten to ask how Mr. Branson found her daycare.

She heard the door creak and open up again. Mr. Branson called, "I forgot to tell you, Scotty's allergic to chocolate milk."

The door shut. Susan rubbed her left cheek, the one he had not kissed. She stared at the meat-child. She felt the kick of queasy memories in her gut, things she could not think about for the life of her.

Allergic to chocolate milk.

She expected to have an easier time lugging Scotty the meat-child into the kitchen. He could not have weighed more than sixty pounds, but felt at least double that. When she lifted him up, legs - which she hadn't seen - uncurled from the thing's red belly. She recoiled, dropping him. She fled to the kitchen and pressed up against the refrigerator. *Take care of the child, take care of the child, take care of the child*, she told herself. *Breathe in, breathe out.*

She returned with oven mitts. She stood over the meat-child, clamping and unclamping the mitts like a cottony lobster.

None of the other children said anything as Susan dragged Scotty into the kitchen by his legs. Susan wondered what the little idiots would tell their parents about Scotty, the new boy. She figured most of them would not remember anything at all. They would recall nothing about meat.

Scotty was too heavy for Susan to lift onto the kitchen table. Instead, she slid him into the corner, beside Tanuki's food and water. She emptied the water bowl, gone green with stagnation, into the sink. She cursed her husband for the empty bottle of Jack he'd left out on the counter. The prick was a drinker these days, ever since the cat died. She understood how much he loved Tanuki. She loved Tanuki too. They had adopted the cat thirteen years ago, before they were even married. Now the cat had been dead for over a year. Leaving food and water out was a means of coping that didn't hurt anyone, but if a parent were to see the empty whiskey bottle and complain to the daycare board, Susan could lose her business.

She tried her best to scrape the grime from the bowl but gave up after a half-assed attempt. She set the bowl on the counter. She searched the fridge for chocolate syrup. She realized it was no use. They were out of milk. She grabbed one of her Atkins chocolate-flavored protein shakes.

It was close enough, right?

Susan popped the tab and poured the thick, brown liquid into the bowl. She set the bowl on the floor next to Scotty. "Drink up," she said, but who was she kidding? She was talking to some fucking meat.

She lifted the bowl and tilted it just enough. A few drops splattered on the meat child's back. Nothing happened, so she poured more. Then she let the whole thing spill.

Still, nothing happened.

Susan left the chocolate-soaked Scotty on the linoleum floor and walked out of the kitchen. She peeked into the living room to make sure the kids were alright. Silent as crabs, the children stared at the television screen. The children seemed no less alive than before, but they had gone red and it wasn't from the movie's glow.

Susan screamed at these *new* children. She collapsed on the floor and choreographed an Ian Curtis nightmare. A very bad...

"Mrs. Mackery," said Charlie, the oldest boy she watched.

Susan looked up. Her insides tightened. A trail of crimson ran from the sofa where Charlie had sat to where he stood. The child gave no indication that he realized he was skinless. *How could he be without skin? How could he be alive?*

"Mrs. Mackery," he said.

"What is it, Charlie?" she said. When facing terrible situations, Susan knew to act normal. Acting normal was the key to overcoming all of life's problems.

"That new boy, he hurt me."

Susan looked at the other children. She looked at the cable box. 1:11 glowed green. How could it be over an hour past noon? Mr. Branson dropped off Scotty around eight. In that time, she had done nothing except drag the meat into the kitchen and pour the chocolate shake over it. Something wasn't right. Susan thought she might call her husband. He took care of every problem.

Something moved in the hallway. She looked at the children again, taking count. One was missing. Who? She registered their faces. Haley.

"Haley," she called, "Haley!"

The toilet flushed. The sink ran for a few seconds, then the bathroom door opened. "Haley," she said.

The thing that scuttled into the living room was not Haley, even if it wore her face. It grinned, but the skull beneath failed to smile in sync with the loosely draped little girl face. Susan imagined more than one mind existing behind that hideous face.

In the kitchen there was a terrible crying, like a cat meowing, hung by its tail from a basketball hoop, swinging like a furry piñata, then beaten with metal bats into a sad and voiceless thing. *Everything and everyone was crying.*

Susan awoke in her bed. The light overhead made her jaw ache. Her husband stood over her. He squinted at her. She felt pitiful and ashamed. He held out his hand and she took it.

"Where are the children?" she said.

He pulled her to her feet. "A new business offer came in so I took the day off. You were passed out like a sorority bitch. I called the parents. The children are gone. They'll be back. Are you hungry? I cooked dinner."

Of course they'll be back, Susan thought. Her guts mumbled. She had eaten nothing all day. "Did you have a bad day?" she said. *Would he ask about her day?*

He kissed her cheek, moving away from her as he did so. He turned off the light on his way out.

No, of course not.

Susan forced herself out of bed. She wanted to explain everything.

When she entered the kitchen, she felt scrambled in a fog. Mr. Branson stood from his seat at the table. "What the hell is he doing here?" she said.

Her husband turned around. "Ted is my partner. We're going into a sort of…new business together."

"What kind of business?" she demanded.

Her husband and Mr. Branson responded together. "Your

new husband," they said.

The doorbell rang and Susan knew she must answer it, if only to escape from her husband and Mr. Branson for a moment or two.

Susan left the kitchen, passed through the lightless living room, and pressed her face against the front door. She looked through the door peephole onto the lit front porch.

Outside stood Tanuki. No, even if it wore the face of their beloved cat, it couldn't be. *It couldn't...not Tanuki, not with his head on the body of a boy.*

The boy's body was bookish and pale, just as Susan always imagined Tanuki.

Tanuki held a platter of meat. All seven of the daycare children stood around him.

"Meow, can we come in now?" Tanuki said. He spoke in the voice of a six-year-old boy with a sore throat.

Susan threw the door open. She looked into the eyes of her dead cat and saw her husband approaching from behind.

Two hands wrapped around her belly.

"It's just me," said her husband. "Don't tense up like that."

She wanted to run away, but there was nowhere to go. Her husband kissed the back of her neck. "What's the matter with you?" he said.

"Nothing."

"Nothing? If nothing's the matter with you, then why the hell are you letting our guests sit outside in the cold? Ask them in for dinner.

"Go on," he said.

She looked at Tanuki and the children. She said, "Would you like to come in for dinner?"

Her husband jerked her inside and waved for Tanuki and the kids to follow. "Tanuki," he said gruffly, "take the kids into the kitchen. I'd like to speak with my wife alone."

Tanuki gave a thumbs up and shuffled into the kitchen. The children followed close behind, as if they feared passing beyond Tanuki's supervision.

Susan was bawling now. Hysterical, even. She was so ashamed of herself, to lose her composure like this. "What the hell's going on?" she said.

Her husband said, "Don't get upset over this. You've got no goddamn reason to get upset. I should slap the shit out of you. I *know* you've wanted us to start our own family for a while now and I've been talking things over with Ted, I said let's do it. Let's start our own family. We needed more money, but Ted said just have a few extra workers. Kids will pay for kids. Ted told me how. I invited him to live with us."

"Slow down," Susan said, starting to gain her composure. "Slow down. Where did you meet Ted? Why did he come here this morning?"

"How did I meet who? Who did I meet?"

"Ted Branson. How did you meet Ted Branson?"

Her husband crossed his arms and head-butted her like a wooden Indian chief. "I met him nowhere special," he said.

Susan buckled over. She pulled her hair. She clawed at her husband's feet. *This is it*, she thought, *I've done it for sure. This knitted little life of mine is gone for good.* "Nowhere special," she sobbed, "nowhere special. For God's sake, what does that mean? Nowhere spe-"

He kicked a dirty Reebok into her *chomp-chomps*, as he had nicknamed the cat's teeth.

She bit her tongue and it burst in half.

"I didn't mean that," her husband said, as Susan gagged up blood.

"Truly, I didn't. All I want is for you to understand that we can finally start a family. I want *you* to be happy. *We* can finally be happy. And if it's really that important to you, I met Ted in a bathroom. He was looking for a daycare service."

Susan looked up at her husband. Was this really her husband? She had always considered him the more rational of the two of them, and while she knew *she* was being irrational, well, he was an abusive spouse!

But then she thought of Tanuki's death, and it hurt far worse than everything he had just done to her.

"Where did Tanuki come from?" she said.

"That's mine and Ted's business," he said.

"Ted and I decided that since Tanuki might have trouble acquiring a job, he's the best candidate for fatherhood. Ted and I will provide financial support while you stay home with Tanuki and the kids. We'll be the perfect family."

In the kitchen, Tanuki's mewing laughter pitched above the kid laughter. *This is not my life*, she thought. *I cannot be Susan. Make me into someone else. I cannot be Susan. I have always been just Susan. Please. Anyone. Make. Me. Into. Someone Else. Anyone. Or someone, come here to me.*

Despite the transformations of her world, she remained stifled, obedient, and afraid. In other words, she remained painfully herself.

Everything grew quiet. Her partially-severed tongue hung over her bottom lip. She let the blood run down her chin.

"It's dinner time," her husband said, standing at the front of the table, but Ted was not out with the dinner yet.

Susan leaned back in the seat opposite end her husband. She looked around at all the fleshless faces. Susan didn't want a family, or maybe she did still want one. Maybe she wanted this one. She didn't know. Nobody knew if they truly belonged to their family because nobody ever chose their family. She still loved her husband, she supposed. Susan also loved Tanuki.

"Dinner's not ready yet," Mr. Branson – Ted – called from the bathroom.

"Is he preparing dinner in the bathroom?" Susan asked. Forming each word hurt.

Tanuki whined about dinner taking too long. Susan's husband told the cat-child that Father Ted would be just a minute. "He is preparing dinner right now," she said.

"What would it be like," she said, "to be in a family I chose to love?"

"You should ask Ted about that one. He's into Hallmark cards."

The children were laughing, but everyone stopped chattering as Ted stepped out of the bathroom carrying a silver platter holding a large rib-eye steak.

"I would like to bless this meal," Ted said. "Bow your heads, everyone."

Susan bowed her head. Ted began a prayer to the meat. *Lord Meat, we thank you for your sacrifice, for transforming our children so that someday we might also come to wear the perfect likeness of you....*

Susan wondered how long her tongue would bleed, and whether, exactly, the hanging part would interfere with her enjoyment of tonight's family dinner.

CRAZY LOVE

So you meet a stranger on the bus. The two of you speed headfirst into small talk about diminishing salmon populations, and that settles it. You will have a casual fuck. Two hours later, you float on the pillows that appear when the storms of good sex have ceased thundering. You're both vigorous cuddlers, so it's hard to tell in the half-light where your flesh ends and the stranger's flesh begins. You fall asleep, very much in love.

The stranger shakes you into wakefulness around seven in the morning and says, "You knocked me up." You insist upon the eternal virtues of prophylactics and tell the stranger to go back to sleep. The stranger gets out of bed and paces from one end of your room to the other. This irritates you. You have always hated pacers and morning people. It seems you have fucked the wrong kind of stranger again.

Five minutes later, the stranger yelps and gives birth to a child. Faithful to its strange origins, the child is a weird-looking thing. It could pass for one of those plush, cutesy-eyed hearts that pop up in grocery stores and boutique shops when February rolls around. You find it hard to imagine that your genes played any role in its creation. "It sure is a weird-looking thing," you say.

"I think it is beautiful," the stranger says, and that settles it. You make coffee and eggs and the three of you take the bus down to the courthouse. You get married. With a child thrown into the equation, you see no option but marriage. Still, you're uncertain whether you really love this spouse-stranger. After all, the spouse-stranger is a pacer and a morning person. You return home from a honeymoon of takeout Chinese and an Italian horror film that the spouse-stranger claims to have seen precisely thirty-six times. "Once for every child born," the spouse-stranger says.

You think this is a lot of children for one person to have, but decide it is better to leave your separate pasts unspoken. You find yourself warming up to the fuzzy infant dozing between the two of you on the sofa. Family life might be okay after all.

A month of swell fucking and many diaper changes goes by. Then one morning at the crack of dawn, the spouse-stranger asks for a divorce. You pull the covers to your chin and say, "I thought we were happy."

"I am happy," the spouse-stranger says, "and I feel like I'm in Hell."

"How can you feel both things at once? What makes you think that?" you ask.

"Oh, a lot of things," says the spouse-stranger, packing a suitcase that belongs to you full of clothes that are yours. The spouse-stranger slams the front door three times on the way out.

You prepare to face the trials of single parenting, but first you sleep until noon. With the spouse-stranger gone, you can finally return to your normal habits. When you wake up, the empty bed saddens you. Prickles of loneliness scratch at your insides and turn your thoughts into some kind of lousy meat. Everything you think seems out of place in your head, dragging you to a new all-time low every minute.

You walk into the kitchen and spot a note on the counter. Your heart beats with the gusto of a Bach symphony. You clear your throat and restrain the great hopes the sight of this ketchup-stained note has bestowed upon you. You hold it between your fingers like a scroll from the heavens and read:

The baby died. I put it in the trash. Remember to pull the can to the curb tomorrow. I'm sorry I don't love you anymore. Don't feel bad about it. This is just what I do.

You pace from one end of the kitchen to the other. You hate yourself during every minute of it, but you're compelled to pace. You're a mad pacer. You were born to pace. The sun shines and you pace. The sun hangs itself on the blue horizon and you pace. The blue horizon fizzles into black emptiness and you pace. Black emptiness and you pace. Black emptiness. Pace.

Morning comes and you pass out on the floor. You dream that you die and meet the spouse-stranger on a bus taking you to Hell. The spouse-stranger shows you a ticket stamped PURGATORY in gold embossment. The bus drives off a cliff and you wake up. You realize what you must do.

You leave your house and stand at the bus stop. The bus pulls up five minutes later. Strangers occupy half the seats. The other seats remain unfilled. You sit beside a stranger near the back of the bus. The two of you speed headfirst into small talk about the poisoned cat food epidemic in China, and that settles it.

You go to the stranger's house because your own house is behind you now. You feel the stranger's stop approach like a historical compendium of all the strangers who have ever slept together.

But when you get to the stranger's house, you find that it is haunted. You stand outside and squint your eyes at the house's twisting spires, as if to gauge its spook count and decide whether the risk is worth the fuck. "I grew up in a few haunted houses," you say.

"It isn't that haunted," the stranger says.

Puffy white ghosts peer out from all the windows. The house is definitely *that* haunted. "Maybe it isn't," you say, and walk inside.

The stranger guides you upstairs to a room where a stained

mattress lies in a corner. "I can't have sheets in the house because the ghosts poop on them," the stranger says.

"That would be a lot of dirty laundry," you say.

You and the stranger undress and lie on your backs. Then you turn and kiss the stranger and you fold over each other. The sex isn't that great because ghosts howl and fly through the walls. Lovemaking strikes you as a funny thing to do in a haunted house and you laugh. The stranger takes sex very seriously and does not laugh. This also makes it less great. The stranger sighs a ghostly wail and orgasms. You haven't come yet, but the stranger says, "I guess that's the end of our sleeping together."

"I guess that's it," you say. You dress in silence, recalling all the reasons you vowed never to live in a haunted house again. A ghost follows you down the stairs on your way out. You wonder if the stranger ever gets lonely and tries to sleep with the ghosts.

You stand at the bus stop and figure you'll have to try again some other day. The bus arrives a few minutes later and you step on. You spot the spouse-stranger you're still legally married to. The spouse-stranger sits beside another stranger who once meant something to you. You can think of nothing that made this stranger different from all the other strangers you have slept with. That stranger was not special, you think. Anyway, it took place in some half-remembered time.

It no longer matters that you engaged in brief encounters with either of these strangers. You still love them, but in the way people love the memory of a carnival funhouse. A gust of longing rises up in you because to hell with it. These encounters do matter. They must add up to something more meaningful than any of the strangers who make them happen. To think otherwise would be sticking a foot in the mouth of your own aimlessness.

Your stop is coming up and you want a stranger to talk with, but all of them converse with other strangers. Your thoughts no longer slosh around like bad meat, but you are hungry and a hamburger sounds delightful. Half a mile from your stop, you stand and tiptoe to the front of the bus. You tap the driver on the shoulder. You think that even if she's a pterodactyl and missing a front tooth, her blue uniform compliments her yellow eyes. You can tell this dinosaur has style and taste.

You ask if she's heard of an all-night diner that recently opened.

"No," she says, bubblegum smacking between her elongated jaws.

Before you can tell her about the dinner and ask her on a date, the pterodactyl misses a turnoff because you're distracting her. The bus zooms straight ahead, right off a cliff. As the bus plummets into a canyon, everybody screams, including your ex-lovers.

The bus driver climbs out of her seat and takes you in her arms. She opens the door and leaps out of the bus. Her wings unfold like a lovely umbrella and you sail toward the sun. Deep down in the canyon, the bus explodes. Those strangers are dead now. It's just you and the pterodactyl. Maybe, if she doesn't have a nest full of babies somewhere, and she doesn't feed you to them, the two of you will hit it off.

Cameron Pierce (glasses) with Jeremy Robert Johnson (beard)

ABOUT THE AUTHOR

Cameron Pierce is the author of Shark Hunting in Paradise Garden, Ass Goblins of Auschwitz, and The Pickled Apocalypse of Pancake Island. He has been a taxidermist's assistant, a paperboy, a shellfish farmer, and a college dropout. He grew up in southern California and lives in Portland, Oregon.

Visit him online at:
www.meatmagick.wordpress.com.

Bizarro books

CATALOG   SPRING 2010

Bizarro Books publishes under the following imprints:

www.rawdogscreamingpress.com

www.eraserheadpress.com

www.afterbirthbooks.com

www.swallowdownpress.com

For all your Bizarro needs visit:

WWW.BIZARROCENTRAL.COM

Introduce yourselves to the bizarro genre and all of its authors with the Bizarro Starter Kit series. Each volume features short novels and short stories by ten of the leading bizarro authors, designed to give you a perfect sampling of the genre for only $5 plus shipping.

BB-0X1
"The Bizarro Starter Kit" (Orange)

Featuring D. Harlan Wilson, Carlton Mellick III, Jeremy Robert Johnson, Kevin L Donihe, Gina Ranalli, Andre Duza, Vincent W. Sakowski, Steve Beard, John Edward Lawson, and Bruce Taylor.

236 pages $5

BB-0X2
"The Bizarro Starter Kit" (Blue)

Featuring Ray Fracalossy, Jeremy C. Shipp, Jordan Krall, Mykle Hansen, Andersen Prunty, Eckhard Gerdes, Bradley Sands, Steve Aylett, Christian TeBordo, and Tony Rauch.

244 pages $5

BB-001"The Kafka Effekt" D. Harlan Wilson - A collection of forty-four irreal short stories loosely written in the vein of Franz Kafka, with more than a pinch of William S. Burroughs sprinkled on top. **211 pages $14**

BB-002 "Satan Burger" Carlton Mellick III - The cult novel that put Carlton Mellick III on the map ... Six punks get jobs at a fast food restaurant owned by the devil in a city violently overpopulated by surreal alien cultures. **236 pages $14**

BB-003 "Some Things Are Better Left Unplugged" Vincent Sakwoski - Join The Man and his Nemesis, the obese tabby, for a nightmare roller coaster ride into this postmodern fantasy. **152 pages $10**

BB-004 "Shall We Gather At the Garden?" Kevin L Donihe - Donihe's Debut novel. Midgets take over the world, The Church of Lionel Richie vs. The Church of the Byrds, plant porn and more! **244 pages $14**

BB-005 "Razor Wire Pubic Hair" Carlton Mellick III - A genderless humandildo is purchased by a razor dominatrix and brought into her nightmarish world of bizarre sex and mutilation. **176 pages $11**

BB-006 "Stranger on the Loose" D. Harlan Wilson - The fiction of Wilson's 2nd collection is planted in the soil of normalcy, but what grows out of that soil is a dark, witty, otherworldly jungle... **228 pages $14**

BB-007 "The Baby Jesus Butt Plug" Carlton Mellick III - Using clones of the Baby Jesus for anal sex will be the hip sex fetish of the future. **92 pages $10**

BB-008 "Fishyfleshed" Carlton Mellick III - The world of the past is an illogical flatland lacking in dimension and color, a sick-scape of crispy squid people wandering the desert for no apparent reason. **260 pages $14**

BB-009 "Dead Bitch Army" Andre Duza - Step into a world filled with racist teenagers, cannibals, 100 warped Uncle Sams, automobiles with razor-sharp teeth, living graffiti, and a pissed-off zombie bitch out for revenge. **344 pages $16**

BB-010 "The Menstruating Mall" Carlton Mellick III - "The Breakfast Club meets Chopping Mall as directed by David Lynch." - Brian Keene **212 pages $12**

BB-011 "Angel Dust Apocalypse" Jeremy Robert Johnson - Meth-heads, man-made monsters, and murderous Neo-Nazis. "Seriously amazing short stories..." - Chuck Palahniuk, author of Fight Club **184 pages $11**

BB-012 "Ocean of Lard" Kevin L Donihe / Carlton Mellick III - A parody of those old Choose Your Own Adventure kid's books about some very odd pirates sailing on a sea made of animal fat. **176 pages $12**

   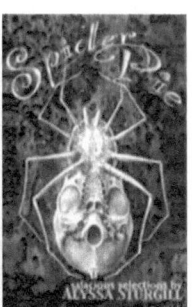

BB-013 "Last Burn in Hell" John Edward Lawson - From his lurid angst-affair with a lesbian music diva to his ascendance as unlikely pop icon the one constant for Kenrick Brimley, official state prison gigolo, is he's got no clue what he's doing. **172 pages $14**

BB-014 "Tangerinephant" Kevin Dole 2 - TV-obsessed aliens have abducted Michael Tangerinephant in this bizarro combination of science fiction, satire, and surrealism. **164 pages $11**

BB-015 "Foop!" Chris Genoa - Strange happenings are going on at Dactyl, Inc, the world's first and only time travel tourism company.

"A surreal pie in the face!" - Christopher Moore **300 pages $14**

BB-016 "Spider Pie" Alyssa Sturgill - A one-way trip down a rabbit hole inhabited by sexual deviants and friendly monsters, fairytale beginnings and hideous endings. **104 pages $11**

BB-017 "The Unauthorized Woman" Efrem Emerson - Enter the world of the inner freak, a landscape populated by the pre-dead and morticioners, by cockroaches and 300-lb robots. **104 pages $11**

BB-018 "Fugue XXIX" Forrest Aguirre - Tales from the fringe of speculative literary fiction where innovative minds dream up the future's uncharted territories while mining forgotten treasures of the past. **220 pages $16**

BB-019 "Pocket Full of Loose Razorblades" John Edward Lawson - A collection of dark bizarro stories. From a giant rectum to a foot-fungus factory to a girl with a biforked tongue. **190 pages $13**

BB-020 "Punk Land" Carlton Mellick III - In the punk version of Heaven, the anarchist utopia is threatened by corporate fascism and only Goblin, Mortician's sperm, and a blue-mohawked female assassin named Shark Girl can stop them. **284 pages $15**

BB-021 "Pseudo-City" D. Harlan Wilson - Pseudo-City exposes what waits in the bathroom stall, under the manhole cover and in the corporate boardroom, all in a way that can only be described as mind-bogglingly irreal. **220 pages $16**

BB-022 "Kafka's Uncle and Other Strange Tales" Bruce Taylor - Anslenot and his giant tarantula (tormentor? fri-end?) wander a desecrated world in this novel and collection of stories from Mr. Magic Realism Himself. **348 pages $17**

BB-023 "Sex and Death In Television Town" Carlton Mellick III - In the old west, a gang of hermaphrodite gunslingers take refuge from a demon plague in Telos: a town where its citizens have televisions instead of heads. **184 pages $12**

BB-024 "It Came From Below The Belt" Bradley Sands - What can Grover Goldstein do when his severed, sentient penis forces him to return to high school and help it win the presidential election? **204 pages $13**

BB-025 **"Sick: An Anthology of Illness" John Lawson, editor** - These Sick stories are horrendous and hilarious dissections of creative minds on the scalpel's edge. **296 pages $16**

BB-026 **"Tempting Disaster" John Lawson, editor** - A shocking and alluring anthology from the fringe that examines our culture's obsession with taboos. **260 pages $16**

BB-027 **"Siren Promised" Jeremy Robert Johnson** - Nominated for the Bram Stoker Award. A potent mix of bad drugs, bad dreams, brutal bad guys, and surreal/incredible art by Alan M. Clark. **190 pages $13**

BB-028 **"Chemical Gardens" Gina Ranalli** - Ro and punk band Green is the Enemy find Kreepkins, a surfer-dude warlock, a vengeful demon, and a Metal Priestess in their way as they try to escape an underground nightmare. **188 pages $13**

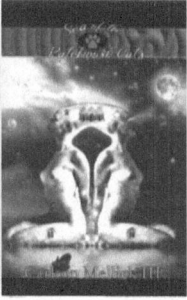

BB-029 **"Jesus Freaks" Andre Duza** - For God so loved the world that he gave his only two begotten sons… and a few million zombies. **400 pages $16**

BB-030 **"Grape City" Kevin L. Donihe** - More Donihe-style comedic bizarro about a demon named Charles who is forced to work a minimum wage job on Earth after Hell goes out of business. **108 pages $10**

BB-031 **"Sea of the Patchwork Cats" Carlton Mellick III** - A quiet dreamlike tale set in the ashes of the human race. For Mellick enthusiasts who also adore The Twilight Zone. **112 pages $10**

BB-032 **"Extinction Journals" Jeremy Robert Johnson** - An uncanny voyage across a newly nuclear America where one man must confront the problems associated with loneliness, insane dieties, radiation, love, and an ever-evolving cockroach suit with a mind of its own. **104 pages $10**

BB-033 **"Meat Puppet Cabaret" Steve Beard** - At last! The secret connection between Jack the Ripper and Princess Diana's death revealed! **240 pages $16 / $30**

BB-034 **"The Greatest Fucking Moment in Sports" Kevin L. Donihe** - In the tradition of the surreal anti-sitcom Get A Life comes a tale of triumph and agape love from the master of comedic bizarro. **108 pages $10**

BB-035 **"The Troublesome Amputee" John Edward Lawson** - Disturbing verse from a man who truly believes nothing is sacred and intends to prove it. **104 pages $9**

BB-036 **"Deity" Vic Mudd** - God (who doesn't like to be called "God") comes down to a typical, suburban, Ohio family for a little vacation—but it doesn't turn out to be as relaxing as He had hoped it would be... **168 pages $12**

  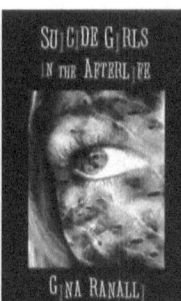 

BB-037 **"The Haunted Vagina" Carlton Mellick III** - It's difficult to love a woman whose vagina is a gateway to the world of the dead. **132 pages $10**

BB-038 **"Tales from the Vinegar Wasteland" Ray Fracalossy** - Witness: a man is slowly losing his face, a neighbor who periodically screams out for no apparent reason, and a house with a room that doesn't actually exist. **240 pages $14**

BB-039 **"Suicide Girls in the Afterlife" Gina Ranalli** - After Pogue commits suicide, she unexpectedly finds herself an unwilling "guest" at a hotel in the Afterlife, where she meets a group of bizarre characters, including a goth Satan, a hippie Jesus, and an alien-human hybrid. **100 pages $9**

BB-040 **"And Your Point Is?" Steve Aylett** - In this follow-up to LINT multiple authors provide critical commentary and essays about Jeff Lint's mind-bending literature. **104 pages $11**

 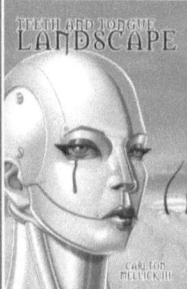  

BB-041 "Not Quite One of the Boys" Vincent Sakowski - While drug-dealer Maxi drinks with Dante in purgatory, God and Satan play a little tri-level chess and do a little bargaining over his business partner, Vinnie, who is still left on earth. **220 pages \$14**

BB-042 "Teeth and Tongue Landscape" Carlton Mellick III - On a planet made out of meat, a socially-obsessive monophobic man tries to find his place amongst the strange creatures and communities that he comes across. **110 pages \$10**

BB-043 "War Slut" Carlton Mellick III - Part "1984," part "Waiting for Godot," and part action horror video game adaptation of John Carpenter's "The Thing." **116 pages \$10**

BB-044 "All Encompassing Trip" Nicole Del Sesto - In a world where coffee is no longer available, the only television shows are reality TV re-runs, and the animals are talking back, Nikki, Amber and a singing Coyote in a do-rag are out to restore the light **308 pages \$15**

BB-045 "Dr. Identity" D. Harlan Wilson - Follow the Dystopian Duo on a killing spree of epic proportions through the irreal postcapitalist city of Bliptown where time ticks sideways, artificial Bug-Eyed Monsters punish citizens for consumer-capitalist lethargy, and ultraviolence is as essential as a daily multivitamin. **208 pages \$15**

BB-046 "The Million-Year Centipede" Eckhard Gerdes - Wakelin, frontman for 'The Hinge,' wrote a poem so prophetic that to ignore it dooms a person to drown in blood. **130 pages \$12**

BB-047 "Sausagey Santa" Carlton Mellick III - A bizarro Christmas tale featuring Santa as a piratey mutant with a body made of sausages. 124 pages \$10

BB-048 "Misadventures in a Thumbnail Universe" Vincent Sakowski - Dive deep into the surreal and satirical realms of neo-classical Blender Fiction, filled with television shoes and flesh-filled skies. **120 pages   \$10**

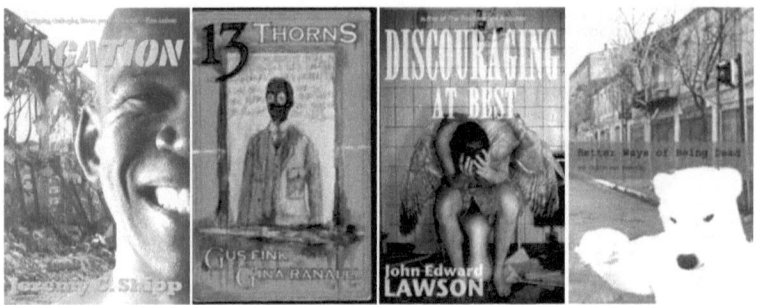

BB-049 **"Vacation" Jeremy C. Shipp** - Blueblood Bernard Johnson leaved his boring life behind to go on The Vacation, a year-long corporate sponsored odyssey. But instead of seeing the world, Bernard is captured by terrorists, becomes a key figure in secret drug wars, and, worse, doesn't once miss his secure American Dream. **160 pages $14**

BB-051 **"13 Thorns" Gina Ranalli** - Thirteen tales of twisted, bizarro horror. **240 pages $13**

BB-050 **"Discouraging at Best" John Edward Lawson** - A collection where the absurdity of the mundane expands exponentially creating a tidal wave that sweeps reason away. For those who enjoy satire, bizarro, or a good old-fashioned slap to the senses. **208 pages $15**

BB-052 **"Better Ways of Being Dead" Christian TeBordo** - In this class, the students have to keep one palm down on the table at all times, and listen to lectures about a panda who speaks Chinese. **216 pages $14**

BB-053 **"Ballad of a Slow Poisoner" Andrew Goldfarb** Millford Mutterwurst sat down on a Tuesday to take his afternoon tea, and made the unpleasant discovery that his elbows were becoming flatter. **128 pages $10**

BB-054 **"Wall of Kiss" Gina Ranalli** - A woman... A wall... Sometimes love blooms in the strangest of places. **108 pages $9**

BB-055 **"HELP! A Bear is Eating Me" Mykle Hansen** - The bizarro, heartwarming, magical tale of poor planning, hubris and severe blood loss... **150 pages $11**

BB-056 **"Piecemeal June" Jordan Krall** - A man falls in love with a living sex doll, but with love comes danger when her creator comes after her with crab-squid assassins. **90 pages $9**

BB-057 **"Laredo" Tony Rauch** - Dreamlike, surreal stories by Tony Rauch. **180 pages $12**

BB-058 **"The Overwhelming Urge" Andersen Prunty** - A collection of bizarro tales by Andersen Prunty. **150 pages $11**

BB-059 **"Adolf in Wonderland" Carlton Mellick III** - A dreamlike adventure that takes a young descendant of Adolf Hitler's design and sends him down the rabbit hole into a world of imperfection and disorder. **180 pages $11**

BB-060 **"Super Cell Anemia" Duncan B. Barlow** - "Unrelentingly bizarre and mysterious, unsettling in all the right ways..." - Brian Evenson. **180 pages $12**

BB-061 **"Ultra Fuckers" Carlton Mellick III** - Absurdist suburban horror about a couple who enter an upper middle class gated community but can't find their way out. **108 pages $9**

BB-062 **"House of Houses" Kevin L. Donihe** - An odd man wants to marry his house. Unfortunately, all of the houses in the world collapse at the same time in the Great House Holocaust. Now he must travel to House Heaven to find his departed fiancee. **172 pages $11**

BB-063 **"Necro Sex Machine" Andre Duza** - The Dead Bitch returns in this follow-up to the bizarro zombie epic Dead Bitch Army. **400 pages $16**

BB-064 **"Squid Pulp Blues" Jordan Krall** - In these three bizarro-noir novellas, the reader is thrown into a world of murderers, drugs made from squid parts, deformed gun-toting veterans, and a mischievous apocalyptic donkey. **204 pages $12**

BB-065 **"Jack and Mr. Grin" Andersen Prunty** - "When Mr. Grin calls you can hear a smile in his voice. Not a warm and friendly smile, but the kind that seizes your spine in fear. You don't need to pay your phone bill to hear it. That smile is in every line of Prunty's prose." - Tom Bradley. **208 pages $12**

BB-066 **"Cybernetrix" Carlton Mellick III** - What would you do if your normal everyday world was slowly mutating into the video game world from Tron? **212 pages $12**

BB-067 **"Lemur" Tom Bradley** - Spencer Sproul is a would-be serial-killing bus boy who can't manage to murder, injure, or even scare anybody. However, there are other ways to do damage to far more people and do it legally... **120 pages $12**

BB-068 **"Cocoon of Terror" Jason Earls** - Decapitated corpses...a sculpture of terror...Zelian's masterpiece, his Cocoon of Terror, will trigger a supernatural disaster for everyone on Earth. **196 pages $14**

BB-069 **"Mother Puncher" Gina Ranalli** - The world has become tragically over-populated and now the government strongly opposes procreation. Ed is employed by the government as a mother-puncher. He doesn't relish his job, but he knows it has to be done and he knows he's the best one to do it. **120 pages $9**

BB-070 **"My Landlady the Lobotomist" Eckhard Gerdes** - The brains of past tenants line the shelves of my boarding house, soaking in a mysterious elixir. One more slip-up and the landlady might just add my frontal lobe to her collection. **116 pages $12**

BB-071 **"CPR for Dummies" Mickey Z.** - This hilarious freakshow at the world's end is the fragmented, sobering debut novel by acclaimed nonfiction author Mickey Z. **216 pages $14**

BB-072 **"Zerostrata" Andersen Prunty** - Hansel Nothing lives in a tree house, suffers from memory loss, has a very eccentric family, and falls in love with a woman who runs naked through the woods every night. **144 pages $11**

BB-073 **"The Egg Man" Carlton Mellick III** - It is a world where humans reproduce like insects. Children are the property of corporations, and having an enormous ten-foot brain implanted into your skull is a grotesque sexual fetish. Mellick's industrial urban dystopia is one of his darkest and grittiest to date. **184 pages $11**

BB-074 **"Shark Hunting in Paradise Garden" Cameron Pierce** - A group of strange humanoid religious fanatics travel back in time to the Garden of Eden to discover it is invested with hundreds of giant flying maneating sharks. **150 pages $10**

BB-075 **"Apeshit" Carlton Mellick III** - Friday the 13th meets Visitor Q. Six hipster teens go to a cabin in the woods inhabited by a deformed killer. An incredibly fucked-up parody of B-horror movies with a bizarro slant. **192 pages $12**

BB-076 **"Rampaging Fuckers of Everything on the Crazy Shitting Planet of the Vomit At smosphere" Mykle Hansen** - 3 bizarro satires. Monster Cocks, Journey to the Center of Agnes Cuddlebottom, and Crazy Shitting Planet. **228 pages $12**

BB-077 **"The Kissing Bug" Daniel Scott Buck** - In the tradition of Roald Dahl, Tim Burton, and Edward Gorey, comes this bizarro anti-war children's story about a bohemian conenose kissing bug who falls in love with a human woman. **116 pages $10**

BB-078 **"MachoPoni" Lotus Rose** - It's My Little Pony... *Bizarro* style! A long time ago Poniworld was split in two. On one side of the Jagged Line is the Pastel Kingdom, a magical land of music, parties, and positivity. On the other side of the Jagged Line is Dark Kingdom inhabited by an army of undead ponies. **148 pages $11**

BB-079 **"The Faggiest Vampire" Carlton Mellick III** - A Roald Dahl-esque children's story about two faggy vampires who partake in a mustache competition to find out which one is truly the faggiest. **104 pages $10**

BB-080 **"Sky Tongues" Gina Ranalli** - The autobiography of Sky Tongues, the biracial hermaphrodite actress with tongues for fingers. Follow her strange life story as she rises from freak to fame. **204 pages $12**

BB-081 **"Washer Mouth" Kevin L. Donihe** - A washing machine becomes human and pursues his dream of meeting his favorite soap opera star. **244 pages $11**

BB-082 **"Shatnerquake" Jeff Burk** - All of the characters ever played by William Shatner are suddenly sucked into our world. Their mission: hunt down and destroy the real William Shatner. **100 pages $10**

BB-083 **"The Cannibals of Candyland" Carlton Mellick III** - There exists a race of cannibals that are made of candy. They live in an underground world made out of candy. One man has dedicated his life to killing them all. **170 pages $11**

BB-084 **"Slub Glub in the Weird World of the Weeping Willows"** **Andrew Goldfarb** - The charming tale of a blue glob named Slub Glub who helps the weeping willows whose tears are flooding the earth. There are also hyenas, ghosts, and a voodoo priest **100 pages $10**

BB-085 **"Super Fetus" Adam Pepper** - Try to abort this fetus and he'll kick your ass! **104 pages $10**

BB-086 **"Fistful of Feet" Jordan Krall** - A bizarro tribute to spaghetti westerns, featuring Cthulhu-worshipping Indians, a woman with four feet, a crazed gunman who is obsessed with sucking on candy, Syphilis-ridden mutants, sexually transmitted tattoos, and a house devoted to the freakiest fetishes. **228 pages $12**

BB-087 **"Ass Goblins of Auschwitz" Cameron Pierce** - It's Monty Python meets Nazi exploitation in a surreal nightmare as can only be imagined by Bizarro author Cameron Pierce. **104 pages $10**

BB-088 **"Silent Weapons for Quiet Wars" Cody Goodfellow** - "This is high-end psychological surrealist horror meets bottom-feeding low-life crime in a techno-thrilling science fiction world full of Lovecraft and magic..." -John Skipp **212 pages $12**

ORDER FORM

TITLES	QTY	PRICE	TOTAL

Please make checks and moneyorders payable to ROSE O'KEEFE / BIZARRO BOOKS in U.S. funds only. Please don't send bad checks! Allow 2-6 weeks for delivery. International orders may take longer. If you'd like to pay online via PAYPAL.COM, send payments to publisher@eraserheadpress.com.

SHIPPING: US ORDERS - $2 for the first book, $1 for each additional book. For priority shipping, add an additional $4. INT'L ORDERS - $5 for the first book, $3 for each additional book. Add an additional $5 per book for global priority shipping.

Send payment to:

BIZARRO BOOKS
C/O Rose O'Keefe
205 NE Bryant
Portland, OR 97211

Address
City   State   Zip
Email   Phone